Six
Spies
in Saranac

Six
Spies
in Saranac

Jack Heinz

Deeds Publishing | Atlanta

Published by Deeds Publishing in Atlanta, GA
www.deedspublishing.com

Printed in The United States of America

Cover design by Mark Babcock.
Cover photograph courtesy of Anne Heinz. Copyright ©2020 Anne Heinz.

ISBN 978-1-950794-19-5

Books are available in quantity for promotional or premium use. For
information, email info@deedspublishing.com.

First Edition, 2020

10 9 8 7 6 5 4 3 2 1

For Ward Just, great novelist and wonderful friend

The boys with their feet on the desks know that the easiest murder case in the world to break is the one somebody tried to get very cute with; the one that really bothers them is the murder someone thought of only two minutes before he pulled it off.

—Raymond Chandler, *The Simple Art of Murder*

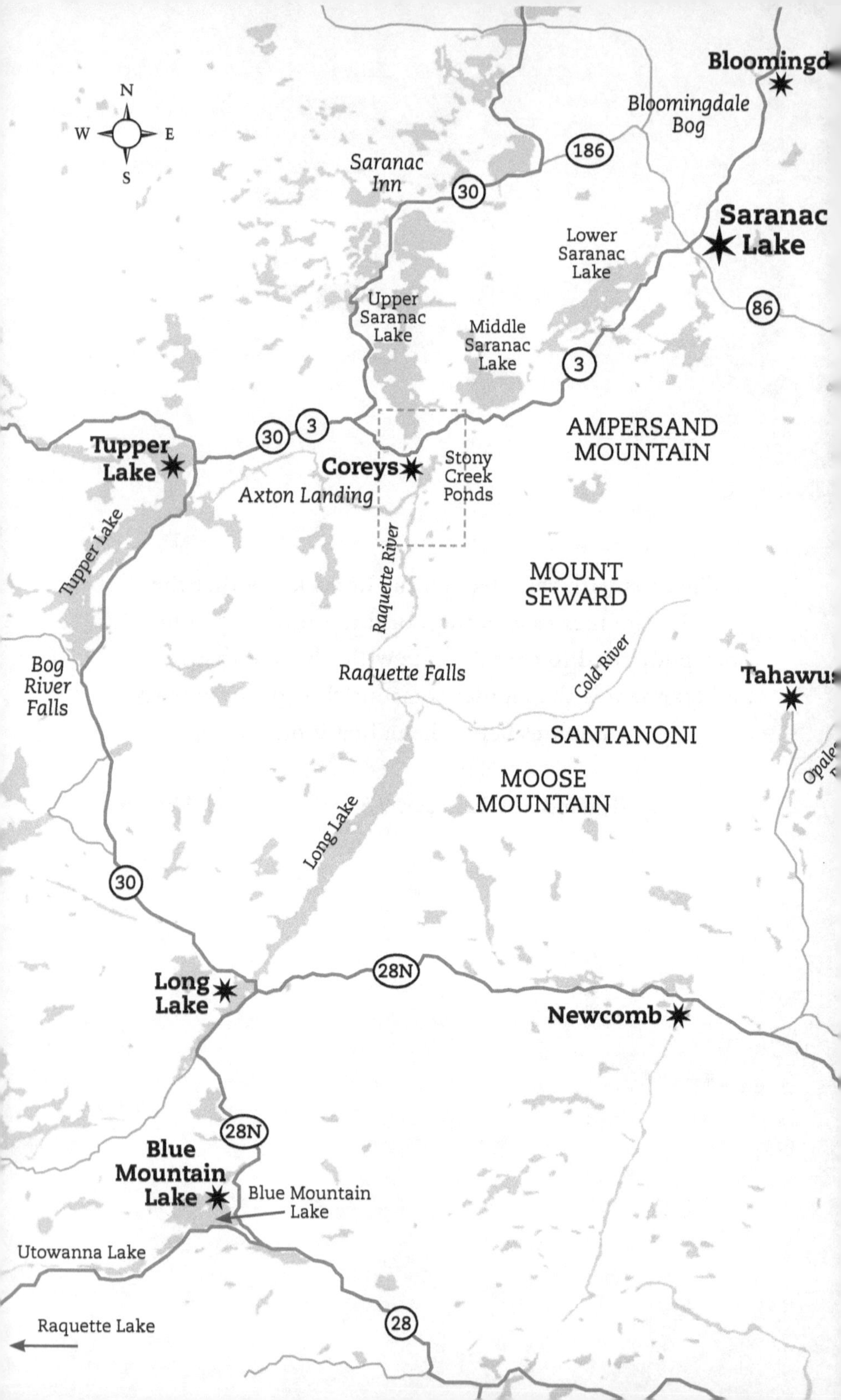

N
W E
S
Bloomingd
Bloomingdale Bog
186
Saranac Inn
30
Lower Saranac Lake
Saranac Lake
86
Upper Saranac Lake
Middle Saranac Lake
3
30 3
AMPERSAND MOUNTAIN
Tupper Lake
Coreys
Stony Creek Ponds
Axton Landing
Tupper Lake
Raquette River
MOUNT SEWARD
Bog River Falls
Raquette Falls
Cold River
Tahawus
SANTANONI
Opale
MOOSE MOUNTAIN
Long Lake
30
28N
Long Lake
Newcomb
28N
Blue Mountain Lake
Blue Mountain Lake
Utowanna Lake
28
Raquette Lake

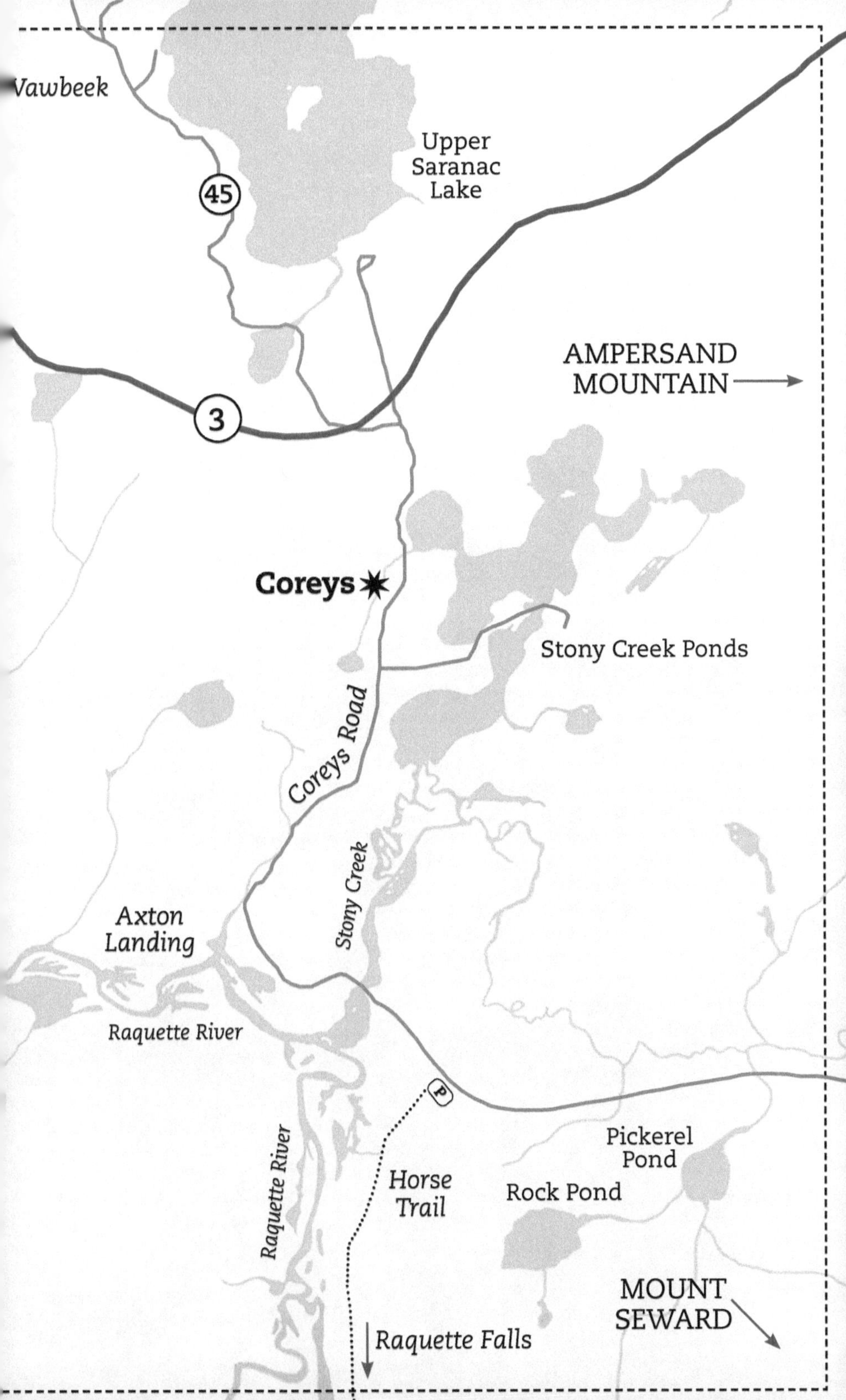

Vawbeek
45
Upper Saranac Lake
AMPERSAND MOUNTAIN →
3
Coreys
Stony Creek Ponds
Coreys Road
Stony Creek
Axton Landing
Raquette River
Raquette River
Horse Trail
Pickerel Pond
Rock Pond
MOUNT SEWARD
Raquette Falls

Chapter One

As soon as you turn off Route 3 onto the Coreys road, the light becomes softer, cooler, greener. The road is narrow and the forest is close on both sides. A hundred yards ahead, around a bend, you have a quick view of open water, one of three small, interlocking lakes called the Stony Creek Ponds. There may be a canoe in the distance—not a motorboat or even a rowboat, a canoe. On the far shore, a trail the Iroquois used to transport furs from the interior of the Adirondacks to traders on the St. Lawrence connects the ponds to the Saranac chain of lakes. In the Adirondacks, a portage is usually called a carry. This one is known as the Indian Carry.

As usual, I had a canoe on top of my car. I parked at the bottom of the hill, untied the canoe, and took it to a launch site down a short path where an inlet runs under the road. A pro carries his canoe into the water. If you care about the boat, you wade until the water is deep enough to float it when you put your weight in it. You don't want to be stuck on the sand. Then you get an opportunity to demonstrate your agility—one foot in the water, you put the other in the middle of the canoe, transfer your weight as you grip both gunwales, and consider your balance. The boat moves as you enter it.

The outlet from the ponds is the Stony Creek. I found it at the far end of the third pond, and from there I traveled downstream to the Raquette River. The creek twists like a snake in pain. The turns, one after another, are disorienting. In an hour or so, the creek, my canoe, and I entered the river a half mile upstream of Axton Landing.

The body was in shallow water, right at the landing. Actually, there isn't much of a landing, but there was a body. There's no dock, no buildings. The place is one of only three take-outs on the Raquette between the villages of Long Lake and Tupper Lake, a distance of forty miles. It's just a sandy beach about ten yards wide with a gradual slope into the water. Voyageurs leave canoes there while they sleep nearby in tents or the lean-to. A canoe is not likely to be stolen at Axton, which is accessible only from the river or by an unpaved, winding road. A small sign marks the turnoff from Coreys Road to a narrow lane, rutted, steep, uneven, that descends to the Raquette, quiet, swift, serene. It doesn't get much casual traffic. If you want privacy, you're unlikely to be seen from either the road or the river. A short walk up the hill is a good place for a picnic—or a murder. There's plenty of foliage to provide cover.

To get to the body, I waded into the water wearing sneakers and jeans. The corpse was face down, the nose and mouth below water. The man—it was surely a man—had to be dead.

I first thought this was likely to be a heart attack from overexertion. Then I saw blood in the water. Not much, but some, and when I turned the body over I found the small, neat hole in the man's forehead. The victim's eyes were open. They looked at me.

In spite of the privacy, Axton is an odd place for a murder. How in the hell would you lure the victim there? First you would need to persuade him to get into a canoe, probably your canoe or one in the same party. He would have to be a friend or acquaintance, but I knew that most murder victims are, in fact, acquainted with their killer. People seldom kill strangers.

Canoes were pulled up on the sand, but there was no one around. The body hadn't been in the water long or the fish would have eaten the eyes. That was bad news. It meant the killer might still be nearby. There were three canoes, which could have carried six men, leaving five who were not lying in the water. How many paddles? Six. Still in the canoes. Good paddles—varnished wood, not plastic. There would be fingerprints on them. Evidence.

I needed to report this before the trail went cold. And what should I do with the body? He was beyond help, but should I pull him out of the water or leave him there? I'd already disturbed the scene. I'd turned him over, and I'd made tracks in the sand. With some caution, not knowing what I might run into, I looked for the campsite of the people who belonged to the three canoes. I found the campsite, but no people. They'd probably gone for a hike—or maybe run for the Canadian border, fifty miles north.

To get to a telephone or get back to my car by water, I'd need to retrace my route, paddling upstream against the current on the Raquette and on the Stony Creek, around all the bends, and then through the ponds. There are forest rangers in the Adirondacks, but I didn't know how to find one. I still don't. They roam around. Because it was summer, a Park caretaker would have been living in the cabin at Raquette Falls, but that's several miles upstream from Axton. It would have taken more than an hour to get there and, when I did, he'd be out patrolling the river. It would be much quicker and closer to walk up the road to the settlement at Coreys, hoping to find one of the summer residents.

That's what I did, and I found Harold Little, known as "Tiny," sitting on his screened porch overlooking the ponds. Tiny is a character, but not an Adirondack character. He's a Midwestern farmer, retired and transplanted. His face, abraded by sun, wind, and insecticides, suggests that he spent fifty years in cornfields. He's tall and rail-thin, friendly, and a man of many words, but the words are oddly chosen. His neighbors call it "Tiny talk."

I had some difficulty getting him to believe what I was telling him. "Well, now, hold your horses there, son. What you're tellin' me is that a man, maybe a Boy Scout I'm thinkin', went swimmin' down at Axton and ran into a heap of trouble, as they say."

"No, what I'm telling you is that he's dead."

"Well, now, how d'ya know that? It could be that he was just restin' sorta like, maybe takin' a short nap."

"No, Mr. Little, he has a bullet hole in the middle of his forehead, and he isn't going anywhere until somebody picks him up and carries him."

"That's hard to believe, I don't mind tellin'. Don't ya see, we've never had any of that." Tiny took his feet off the table. "A bullet hole you say! Can't be. In the huntin' season, they'll be some bullet wounds then maybe, but that's not for a couple of months yet."

"Mr. Little, do you have a telephone?"

"Why yes, indeed, of course I have a telephone. A kind man from the Bell Trust came out here and brought me a new one not too long ago. Said it would cost me only pennies a day. A great convenience," he said.

"I'd like to call the sheriff at Tupper Lake."

"I don't know the sheriff in Tupper."

"Can I use your telephone?"

"Yes, of course, you're only too welcome, of course. But don't ya think before we do that, maybe we should take my Caddy and just mosey down to Axton to check it out, sorta like. Before we go about haulin' the sheriff out and ruinin' his day, poor thing. We could just fire up the little darlin' and take a pleasant drive down the Coreys Road to Axton."

I called the sheriff.

We didn't fire up the little darlin', the sheriff in due course arrived, and the man was still in the river, just as I had left him. The campsite was still deserted, but the campers arrived back a couple of hours later and found their tents and canoes surrounded by orange crime-scene tape. By that time, the state police were there, including evidence technicians.

It turned out that the campers were from Rochester, three middle-aged couples — a hardware store owner, an accountant, a dental hygienist, an undertaker, and two schoolteachers. I'm not sure how those occupations were distributed across the couples. I don't remember. The canoes and paddles were theirs. They hadn't seen or heard anything, or so they said. They seemed credible. So the killing must have taken place after they had arrived and had gone on their hike. They would surely have seen the body when they landed their canoes.

The undertaker took a professional interest in the proceedings, but he was shooed away. I was shooed away too, which was a good thing, but not before the police had taken some interest in me. My cover, as a captain in the Air Force, held up. I'm sure that when the paperwork got to the FBI they knew better, but they kept quiet. As a formal matter, I'm assigned to a slot as a protocol officer on the staff of the Secretary of the Air Force, but I take my orders from the CIA's domestic operations section, headquartered at Langley. To make it all more legit, I do, in fact, have an Air Force commission, and anyone who gets into the Department of Defense records will find me there. I don't often wear a uniform, but I keep one nearby.

* * *

It was the summer of 1964. The Cold War was hot. The summer before, the Soviets had put missiles in Cuba aimed at the White House, the Pentagon, and the Capitol; the Vietnam War was starting to heat up; Students for a Democratic Society (the student anti-war protest organization) had held its first convention and had issued the "Port Huron statement," a manifesto; Dr. King and Ralph Abernathy had staged their march on Washington; the Soviets had detonated a fifty-megaton hydrogen bomb; and we had tried to invade the Bay of Pigs, and failed. It was a busy time.

But I was on assignment in the wilderness. I went to high school in Saranac Lake, only about fifteen miles from Axton, and Langley sent me here because we had a problem at the titanium mine at Tahawus. I was investigating. My CIA training covered codes, surveillance, eavesdropping, and general skullduggery, but I'm not a homicide cop. I know some self-defense moves, and a weapon is available to me if I need it, but I don't usually carry one. That day at Axton, I was trying to remember where I had left it. In a safe at the Pentagon, I thought. Or maybe Langley.

So far I didn't really know that the dead man had any connection to the titanium mine, but the thought had occurred to me. There's a trail running from Axton to Tahawus. It goes south along the Raquette River, bypassing the Seward mountain range, then east along the Cold River and past Santanoni Mountain and Moose Mountain to the mine, which is just west of the

Boreas range. It's a long walk, but the dead man and his killer could have hiked to Axton from Tahawus. People do it. More likely, they took the river, coming downstream in a canoe from Long Lake, past the falls. If they did, the killer probably made his escape by continuing downstream to the village of Tupper Lake or beyond. He'd be long gone. Of course, it was possible that the two of them had driven from anywhere and then walked down to the river and transacted their fatal business, after which the murderer just went back up the path to the car and drove away. That would've been even easier, but more likely to be seen. Tiny Little and his neighbors might have noted the car. And why would a murderer have picked Axton and bothered to walk down to the landing?

I needed to contact Rabbit. Rabbit is a man named Charles Maranville, the director of domestic operations at the Agency. He was in Navy Intelligence during the war, and General "Wild Bill" Donovan spotted him there and recruited him when the CIA evolved out of the Office of Strategic Services (OSS). Rabbit is from Chicago and went to Princeton. He knew Adlai Stevenson there, another Princeton old boy from Illinois, and he was a corporate lawyer, but he's called Rabbit because there was a famous baseball player named Rabbit Maranville. The people at the CIA seem to think this is logical. They are freethinkers.

To report to Rabbit, I needed to use a telephone that was unlikely to be tapped. The lines at Langley are constantly monitored for taps, but that can't be done for many of the phones that call in, and a scrambler was too heavy and bulky to transport. The phone in my room at the hotel wasn't an option because calls went through an operator and she could listen if she wanted to. So the best choice was a public telephone booth. For this report, I used the one at the Saranac Lake post office. For the next call, I'd use a different phone.

"Rabbit, Joe Boudreau reporting from Saranac."

"Any developments?"

"Well, I'm not sure yet. There was some drama today, but it may or may not be our business. There was a body in the Raquette River, but I don't know who he is. I found the body pretty far downstream from the mine, closer to Tupper Lake. I don't think I'd ever seen the man before. I didn't want to disturb it as much as I would have had to for a thorough search, but I stuck around the scene until the police pulled him out of the river and went through his pockets. They didn't find anything. He was clean, or had been picked clean."

"How'd he die?"

"He had a well-placed hole in the middle of his forehead. One wound."

"Sounds professional."

"Possibly. Or maybe just lucky."

"What makes you think it has anything to do with the mine?"

"Supposition. People don't get shot in the middle of their foreheads around here, and there's a hiking trail from where I found him to Tahawus."

"Right. Well, keep on it. See if you can find out who he is."

I wanted Rabbit to tell me how hard I should push this, so I said, "If we want a thorough search of the body, looking for microfilm, taking his shoes apart and so on, we'd need to intervene officially to get that. Otherwise, they'll just do their usual job."

"I'd rather not intervene if we don't have to. Local police departments can be pretty leaky. I don't want talk that tells the KGB we're watching. Speaking of watching, where's the man we've been interested in?"

"I don't know. I've been looking for him. The last I knew, he was at the mine. He hasn't shown up in Saranac or Tupper, but there's a lot of territory here. It's possible he knows we're on to him. It's hard to nose around without having it get back to him."

"Tradecraft, Joe, tradecraft."

I laughed. "I'll try to remember that. I'll wear one of my fake mustaches."

"OK. Just keep me informed."

"I'll do it."

* * *

I was staying at the old Hotel Saranac in a small room high enough up to have a view of the hills. The place is a bit down at the heels, but it's convenient. There's a lighted sign, a big one, on the roof. It says "Hotel Saranac," but the electric connections only work for the first half of each word, so at night it says "Hot Sara". People in town like it that way, and it attracts some interesting customers.

Some of the Saranac folks remembered me from my high school days. In town, I sometimes wore my uniform. I told myself that it reinforced my cover, and it got me free coffee at the Full Moon. When high school friends asked what I was doing back in Saranac, I mumbled something about Griffiss Air Force Base down at Rome. I don't know why I would have been staying in Saranac if I had business at Rome, but that didn't seem to bother them. Or maybe they were just too polite to ask. Air Force guys don't seem like hotdogs in a town full of ski jumpers and bobsledders.

One problem with wearing my uniform is that I forget to salute. Since I don't wear it often, I'm not expecting salutes, but if I run into an enlisted man who salutes me I need to wake up and return the gesture. It's even worse when I see a superior officer. Fortunately, there weren't many of those in Saranac. If I failed to salute a superior, that could cause embarrassment, at best. Curiosity would not be good. This is a reason to stick with civilian clothes. Absentmindedness is not generally desirable in a spy, but a certain amount of unpredictable behavior can be helpful. Awkwardness—forgetfulness and tripping over things—puts them off their guard. In the trade, we refer to it as "the Inspector Clouseau effect."

* * *

On Monday morning, I drove from Saranac to Tupper to see the sheriff, to find out whether the Axton floater had been identified. Tupper is very different from Saranac. Saranac is artsy—lots of watercolorists and musicians, flower children, graphic designers, and retired professors. Tupper is more gritty. Its high school teams are called the Lumberjacks. Logs used to be floated downriver from Tupper to mills on the St. Lawrence. That's over now. But it's still a blue-collar town; Saranac is tie-dyed.

As Route 3 enters Tupper, you see on the right at least two square blocks of institutional buildings, all painted white. That was once a TB hospital. Now they struggle to find another use for it. Before and after World War I, people suffering from consumption came to the mountains for a cure—the clean, cool air was good for their lungs. Apart from the old sanatorium, though, there isn't much to see in Tupper. Neither lumber nor TB is the money-maker it once was. The main street has a movie theater, and a block down from the theater is the local office of the county sheriff. I introduced myself to the deputy in charge.

"Good morning, officer. I'm Joe Boudreau. I was wondering whether you've identified the man who was found at Axton Landing."

"Boudreau? I was a good friend of the late Ted Boudreau, who passed on last year."

"Ted was my uncle. A nice man."

"Yes. A nice guy and a fine carpenter. You have a lot of cousins around here—there are as many Boudreaus in these hills as there are deer."

"Not quite, not quite."

"I'm Hank Day." The officer offered his hand and I shook it. "It's a murder investigation that you're asking about. Could I see some identification?"

I showed him my service ID.

"Oh! *Captain* Boudreau. I'm sorry, I didn't realize it without your uniform."

"That's OK. I'm off-duty today, and let's just make it Joe."

"Fine by me. Call me Hank. To answer your question, we don't know who the man from Axton is. No prints on file, but we're getting a lot of interest in that question."

"What kind of interest?"

"We got an inquiry from Washington, D.C., from the FBI."

That surprised me, so I asked, "Why is the FBI into it?"

"Don't know. The State Police up in Malone are handling it now. For that matter, Joe, what's your interest in the case? Is it official?"

"No, I'm just curious because I'm the guy who found the body and reported the death."

"I thought Tiny Little reported it. The call came in from his phone number."

"Yeah. The phone was at his house. But I made the call."

"So what's Captain Boudreau doing at Axton? What brings you to these parts?"

"Just visiting family and friends. I went to high school in Saranac, so I'm staying there for a spell, seeing people. I've got some business down at Rome."

"You stationed at Rome now?"

"No, I'm at the Pentagon."

"Oh, the Pentagon. With the mukkety-mucks."

"Yeah, but at the Pentagon captains are sent out for coffee." Officer Day laughed.

* * *

I decided that I needed to get Rabbit involved to find out why the FBI was bothering with this. I did, Rabbit made some calls, and the story was that the Soviet Embassy in D.C. was missing a man. One of their military attachés, one Pavel Kuznetsov, hadn't been seen for several days, and the Soviets had asked the FBI to help find him.

I said to Rabbit, "If the Soviets thought their guy had defected to us, would they ask the FBI to track him down?"

"Not ordinarily. The first thing they'd do is send out a hit squad to find him and terminate him. But it's possible it was a feeler to see if we already had him. Or maybe they actually just wanted help. I think it's likely that they don't know where he is and they want to locate him, or they're worried that something bad happened to him. But here's the interesting thing: The Russkies told the FBI that Kuznetsov might be in the Adirondack Mountains. Why? Why did they think he might be where you are?"

"It kind of fits, doesn't it?"

"Yes, it does."

Here's the reason it fit. Two weeks earlier I was watching a guy employed at the titanium mine as a draftsman, a twenty-eight year old named Bill Reilly. I saw him having lunch at Little Italy in Tupper, alone. He read a book as he ate. After lunch he walked two blocks to the old synagogue, a lovely historic building, and he posted an advertisement for a rock concert on the bulletin board there. Then he drove to the southeast corner of town to the Jewish cemetery.

I was watching through high-powered binoculars, posing as a bird-watcher. Reilly walked into the cemetery, removed a loose stone at the base of the Gewertz monument, took some papers out of his book, put them into the gap where the stone had been, and replaced the stone. Then he left. My problem was to get what he deposited, not be seen doing it, copy the papers, and return them before his contact checked the dead letter box. That was a little dicey because, as he was leaving, Reilly saw me out on the road with my bird-watching glasses. But bird-watchers in the Adirondacks are not unusual.

It would be unusual, however, to advertise a rock concert to the elderly ladies at the synagogue. So I figured the ad was a signal to his contact that the box was filled. If I took the signal down for twenty-four hours, it might give me time to remove the drop and copy it. But if the contact was watching the bulletin board, and he saw the signal going up and down, disappearing and then reappearing, it would be suspicious. I hoped he'd think that the ladies who tended the synagogue didn't like rock concerts, and that they took it down. The events posted there were usually chamber music or singers of showtunes. I couldn't do a round-the-clock stakeout on the synagogue because I didn't have anyone to spell me. So I removed the ad.

I put it back up the next day, after taking the message from the Gewertz monument. There was an envelope, sealed. At the Agency, the expert who taught how to open things carefully and then reseal them had worked at the Met restoring etchings. She said the CIA paid better. I did a pretty damn good job of it. The only thing in the envelope was a small strip of microfilm, which I copied and sent to Langley.

Then, of course, I had to get the envelope with the film back into the monument, and someone, either Reilly or his buddies, might be watching the cemetery. Doing it in the daytime would be less suspicious, but a nighttime visit would be less likely to be observed — except that I'd need to find the Gewertz plot in the dark. I could use a small flashlight, but that would be easy to spot from a considerable distance, or I could use night-vision goggles, which are pretty hard to explain away if you're found wearing them. I opted for the flashlight.

The cemetery is surrounded by a handsome cast iron fence with a gate, a closed gate. Would the gate be locked? It wasn't. I'm not enthusiastic about climbing over five-foot fences. Now, where was the Gewertz monument? As I remembered the place, it was in the northeast corner of the cemetery. I used the flash-light, probably too much. I read the headstones. I didn't see Gewertz. I should have made notes. Do I need to carry a note-book and a pencil? That seems tacky. Did James Bond carry a notebook?

Where was Gewertz? I hurried, too much. I could see the headstones, but what I didn't see was that some of the graves also had a small stone at the foot of the plot. I tripped over one, fell, and almost hit my head on a monument. A man found un-conscious in the cemetery with a lump on his head... I'd have to invent a good story. Probably a vicious assailant. But, as it turned out, the monument that almost did me in was Gewertz. This is known as dead reckoning.

The envelope went back into the dead letter box, the rock concert went back up at the synagogue, and I soon received a reply from Rabbit. The microfilm had scientific data and a diagram or a map that was identified by experts at the Pentagon as the layout of old mine tunnels. But the titanium mine was an open pit, not one with tunnels.

Titanium is the metal with the highest strength-to-weight ratio. It's forty-five percent lighter than steel but just as strong. The new TFX (i.e., "tactical fighter experimental") would make unprecedented use of titanium components so that the plane would be able to carry serious armament and electronics but be light enough to take off and land on an aircraft carrier. The plane would be impressively expensive, but taxpayers love to support the national defense budget.

I didn't know at the time, but I know now, that the principal ore for the metallic titanium that would be used in the TFX didn't come from Tahawus, but there was a secure laboratory at the mine that did highly classified research—on exactly what, I don't know. A month before, military intelligence had intercepted Soviet messages that included information about titanium, classified data related to the design of the TFX. The Pentagon was nervous. They wanted to know who the mole was. The microfilm appeared to be related material.

I'd been watching Bill Reilly because he was known to be a red. He was active in the Students for a Democratic Society at SUNY Albany and he was also in the Progressive Labor Party, a Communist front. So Rabbit sent me to the Adirondacks to watch him (and one or two other possible suspects). I know the territory.

Chapter Two

I'd just turned thirty. After training, my first years at the Agency were devoted to tracking reds in Germany. I could never figure out why we gave a damn about German reds, but I guess the U. S. taxpayers wanted to pay for that too. And then I said something that upset our dear German friends—probably something about Sachsenhausen, or Buchenwald, or Auschwitz. So I was sent back to the States and assigned to domestic operations. There seemed to be a feeling that a moron who didn't have enough sense to keep his mouth shut would fit in better in the U. S. of A.

It's lonely work being a spy. The job makes it hard to have close friends, or keep them. Marriage can be a good cover, but your wife has to be in on it, and not many wives would want to do that. And they'd have to be cleared. I've had some girlfriends. A few of them special. But there always came a time when there was a "need to know" problem. My schedule was strange, with unexplained trips and odd telephone calls when I spoke quietly, and they thought I had peculiar friends. The people who were around were peculiar alright, but they weren't friends. The girls knew it didn't smell right. One of them thought I was in the numbers racket. I'd have felt better if she'd thought I was in the CIA. But I wasn't glamorous enough for that. Oh well.

I wanted companionship. Sex wouldn't have been bad either. Linda Coyle was working as a waitress at the Full Moon.

She's too well-educated for that job, but jobs were scarce in Saranac. Linda was two years ahead of me in high school, but she's only a year and a half older. We were in the school play together—"You Can't Take it With You," a classic. I played Mr. De Pinna, who made fireworks down in the basement, and she played Essie, one of the daughters, an awkward ballerina. We liked each other—in real life. I wouldn't put it more strongly than that, but we were friendly. Linda was a star on the high school tennis team. The two of us played a few times, but she always beat me and neither one of us enjoyed that much. She was a risk-taker. I was the slow and steady one; she was impulsive. And she had a big serve. Occasionally, when she was overreaching, I would score a point or two. Linda came back to Saranac after a brief marriage. She had a kid, a boy, four years old. She went to SUNY Canton and then started graduate school in history at Syracuse, but she dropped out to get married. It didn't work out.

She was very good-looking—about five seven, slim, good body, green eyes, dark hair, almost black, quick smile, easy-going. The guy she married made a big mistake, losing her. He's a lawyer, apparently more interested in money than he was in her. Definitely a big mistake. But was catching bad guys or protecting the national security any better? Better than money, better than love?

I was going to the Full Moon more often. Linda helped me figure out the seating pattern so I could sit where she could wait on me, but our conversations were getting to be so long that the management told her to pay some attention to other tables. I didn't want to jeopardize her employment. So I took her out instead. We went to the movie in Tupper. The movie wasn't great, but the time in the car afterwards was highly satisfactory, educational, radical. The babysitter thought that we got home pretty late. Linda's parents still live in Saranac, so her son, William, sometimes went to their house for an overnight. Things were progressing.

* * *

In the daytime, I wondered why the killing was done at Axton. It's certainly off the beaten path. Either the victim or the killer probably knew the place — had been there before. I thought that should narrow the field.

Five days after I found the body at Axton I made another call to Langley. Here is the transcript made from their recording of it. CM is Charles Maranville, Rabbit's official name.

JB: "Rabbit, Joe Boudreau here. I could use some more information, if we have it. What is the enemy after at the mine? What's their objective? That would help me know what to look for."

CM: "Yes, I'm sure it would be helpful. But we don't know. Not yet."

JB: "They must want something specific. What're they trying to accomplish? It's not just a general fishing expedition."

CM: "Presumably they know why they're doing it. We don't, and they aren't talking. But there's important news. The dead man has been identified as Pavel Kuznetsov, the missing military attaché."

JB: "Aha! My nose was correct."

CM: "Yes, but here's the part you're going to like best — the Russkies have nominated you as his killer."

JB: "I didn't even know he was here. I'd never seen him until I found him dead."

CM: "But they don't know that and they wouldn't believe it."

JB: "Oh, great. Why would I kill him?"

CM: "Because you thought he was the enemy, I suppose. Kuznetsov was KGB; we've confirmed that."

JB: "How did they know I'm here?"

CM: "They're good. Have you been careless?"

JB: "I don't think so."

CM: "Well, their embassy has sent a man to Malone 'to pick up the body.' Or so they say. Watch yourself. The guy they've sent will surely be KGB, and he may have some heat with him. I don't know how angry they are. They take care of their own."

JB: "What do we know about Kuznetsov?"

CM: "We're working on that. We're checking all of our sources to trace his history. So far I only know that he was at their embassy in the UK a few years ago—his title was 'second secretary.' The military attaché job here was obviously just a cover. MI6 has a file on him. Not much in it. They say he ran a string of agents."

JB: "I think my sidearm is at the Pentagon. I'll stop in at a sporting goods store and pick one up."

CM: "I recommend you do that. Stay in touch."

* * *

A day later, I received a pre-arranged call from Rabbit to the phone booth at the YMCA. He gave me the latest news. "One of our assets in Russia tells us that the Soviets have design details for the TFX, details classified beyond Top Secret. The Pentagon is very unhappy."

"Would someone who works at the mine have access to those specs?"

Rabbit hesitated. "He shouldn't. But it depends on what files he can get his hands on."

"What kind of data is it?"

"That information is *very* tightly restricted. Even the name of the process is on a need-to-know basis because it's a scientific name and the name reveals something about it. I was told it, but it didn't mean anything to me. They said it would mean something to a person who isn't an ignoramus."

"Well, would a draftsman have the data?"

Again, Rabbit hesitated. I wondered whether he had someone in the room with him. He might have. "I'm told that if he has a good science education, he might pick up stuff that would be revealing."

"Damn! That's not very helpful or informative." I paused. "OK, does the secret have something to do with titanium?"

"They say it's related to the research going on at the lab."

"Could the data be coming from somewhere else?"

"Sure. There are officers in the Pentagon who have all of it. No doubt there are also people at General Dynamics and probably at Boeing."

"Can we rule them out?"

"No, of course not. We're looking at all of them. You're not the only agent working on this. But you're the only one where a KGB man has been killed in immediate proximity."

"I get it." Then I asked, "Why would the KGB kill their own man?"

"Presumably they didn't, but that's what you're supposed to investigate. They say they think you did it. Maybe they really believe that. They're also pressing the FBI and the New York state cops to investigate. If KGB did it, they're putting on a pretty good act."

"They're certainly capable of that."

"Yes, they are."

"I'll stay on it."

"Mind your back."

* * *

I needed help. I had to watch Bill Reilly, but I also needed to track the movements of Pavel Kuznetsov in the days and weeks before he was killed. The Soviet embassy told the FBI that charges on a credit card issued to Kuznetsov had been made at the Adirondack Hotel in Long Lake, located about twenty miles west of Tahawus on what passes for a main road.

So I went to Long Lake, to the hotel, with a small photograph of Kuznetsov that came from the MI6 file. (Why didn't we have our own pictures? Budget cuts? Incompetence?) The lady at the desk was a grandmotherly type, white hair, 65 or 70, a bit vague, but she recognized him.

"Oh yes, that's Dr. Lien. We were sorry to hear the sad news."

"What did you hear?"

"Well, we heard that he died."

"Yes, that's true. Did you read about it in the newspaper?"

"No, a gentleman came here and told us. We had all been very puzzled and concerned. Dr. Lien just disappeared without checking out and all of his clothes and things were still in his room, and we didn't know what had happened to him."

"Ah, I see. Are his clothes still here?"

"No, the gentleman who came picked them up and paid his bill."

"When was that?"

"Oh, two days ago, I believe. Why do you ask?"

"Dr. Lien was an associate of mine. Did the gentleman who paid the bill identify himself?"

"I have his name written down here somewhere." She looked for it. "Here it is! George Spelvin."

I knew that George Spelvin is a name commonly used in theater programs when an actor plays more than one role. His second appearance is listed as George Spelvin.

I said, "I don't think I know Mr. Spelvin. What could you tell me about him?"

"Well, let's see. Nice looking man. Tall. About forty years old, I think. He had a foreign accent like Dr. Lien, a German accent I suppose."

"Yes, maybe so. Or do you think it might have been a Russian accent?"

"I wouldn't know about that. I don't think I'd recognize a Russian accent." She paused. "What would a Russian be doing here?"

"Well, travel is broadening, you know. And this is a beautiful part of the woods."

"Yes, indeed it is."

"One more question, and thank you for your time. How long did Dr. Lien stay here?"

"Oh, about ten days, before he disappeared. I could look it up for you." She looked through the register. "I have it here. Heinrich Lien. He had the room for two weeks but he missed the last three days of that."

"Did he have many visitors?"

"I don't recall visitors, but I wouldn't necessarily have known that." She hesitated. "Wait, now, he liked our Friday fish fry, and the first Friday he was here he said he wanted to be sure to have it again and a younger man joined him that time."

"Did you know the younger man?"

"No, I didn't."

"How much younger, do you think?"

"Oh, considerably younger, but I wouldn't guess his age."

"You've been very helpful, thank you. And thank you for your kindness to Dr. Lien."

* * *

I reported to Rabbit. The reception wasn't great, maybe because of the mountains, but it worked. "I went to the Adirondack Hotel in Long Lake and interviewed the desk clerk, who was probably also the manager. She IDed a photo of Kuznetsov as Dr. Heinrich Lien, who had been a guest at the hotel. She already knew he was dead. Somebody beat me there. Got there a couple of days before me."

"Did she know how he died?"

"I don't think so, and I didn't tell her. I also didn't tell her his real identity. Speaking of identity, here's an interesting puzzle. The man who beat me to the hotel, and paid Kuznetsov's bill and picked up the clothes and personal effects left in the room, gave his name as George Spelvin."

"The theater name?"

"Yeah."

"That's very clumsy. Very obvious. Doesn't sound like the KGB."

"Unless they wanted to be clumsy, obvious. But why would they do that?"

Rabbit didn't think it was KGB style. "Maybe it wasn't the KGB."

"Who else would it be?" I shouldn't have asked that.

He said what I should have known. "Anyone who wanted what might have been hidden with his things. At the very least, of course, he had some way to communicate, probably a radio transmitter."

"Surely it wasn't the FBI, but maybe we should ask them."

Rabbit agreed. "I'll do that. I'll also do a search on Dr. Heinrich Lien to see if we have anything on that name. How long did he stay at the hotel?"

"About eleven or twelve days—until he died."

"That's long enough to have several meetings with somebody."

I thought of Reilly, of course. "I've got a lead I'll pursue."

"I think maybe the KGB is playing with us. Cat and mouse."

"But why would they want to attract attention?"

Rabbit didn't have a theory. "Good question. Stay on it."

"Will do."

Chapter Three

As I was having a cup of coffee and reading the *New York Times* at the Full Moon, a distinguished-looking, middle-aged man in a handsome tweed jacket approached my table. He stopped.

"Captain Boudreau, I believe?"

He spoke with a British accent, what they call plummy, probably Oxford or Cambridge.

"Yes, I'm Joe Boudreau."

"May I join you? I'd like to have a brief word. Won't take a moment."

"Sure. Please sit down."

He did. "You and I are in the same line of work, Captain."

"Oh, are you a military officer?"

"That wasn't the work I had in mind." He laid both of his hands flat on the table. So I could see them, I suppose. It was a gesture of openness. He then said, "I understand you found a man's body in the river. The company I work for is very eager to identify the person responsible for his death."

I replied. "I understand. I'd like to do that too."

"But you were there, Mr. Boudreau." He dropped the "Captain." "Would you mind telling me how you happened to be there? It is all rather 'convenient.' Or so it seems to us." You could hear the quotation marks around the word convenient.

"Before we get into questions, you've not yet introduced yourself. What name are you using today?"

He laughed. A small laugh. "Forgive me. I'm forgetting my manners." He bent over, and I could see the bulge under his tweed jacket. A shoulder holster. I suspect that the glimpse was intentional. "I'm Ev Hastings."

"And would the Ev be short for Everett?"

"I suppose the Ev could be short for Everett." A short pause. "In this case, however, it is not. My Christian name is Evelyn, a fact that your fellow countrymen seem to regard with amusement. So let's just make it Ev. And I know that your name is, in fact, Boudreau and that you are a member of the rather large clan of Adirondack Boudreaus. An almost Scottish sort of thing. So I will do you the courtesy of telling you that I am, in fact, named Hastings — which will no doubt be confirmed by your friends in Virginia. I believe they have a file on me. Indeed, I'm told that I have a reputation.… Now, with that out of the way, let's return to my question. How did you happen to be at the scene of Colonel Kuznetsov's death?"

I didn't like his arrogance, so I was dismissive, which was a mistake. "I was enjoying nature. Axton is on a nice, quiet stretch of the river."

"Oh, come now, Joe, I've been kind to you. You can do better than that. Let's try again."

I considered that. "Fair enough. I was engaged in my work, which you probably know as well as I do."

"There must be some honor in this business, Joe. Did you kill him? Perhaps you had good reason."

"No, I didn't. Why would I do that?"

"Well, as a premise, let us say because Colonel Kuznetsov was engaged in stealing the secrets of your government, your employer, a perfectly good reason to kill him, a traditional reason."

"If I'd known he was stealing secrets, I could have had him deported. I wouldn't have needed to kill him."

"But that might not have frightened the source of the data."

"Well, in fact, I didn't know what he was doing. I didn't even know who he was when I found him."

"Perhaps you knew him as Dr. Heinrich Lien."

"I know that name now. I didn't know it then. I'd never even seen him until I saw him dead."

"I think that's probably true. Mr. Harold Little tells me that you seemed upset and confused when you came to him after you found the body. Mr. Little, by the way, is an interesting chap. Our conversation was lengthy, as this interview threatens to be. So permit me to help you recall why you were at the Axton landing that afternoon. I suggest you were there because you were looking for, or perhaps tracking, a young man named Bill Reilly. Does that refresh your recollection?"

"The same Bill Reilly who works for you?"

"Answer the question." Hastings stared at me, hard.

"Yes, I was looking for Bill Reilly."

"We know you've been watching Reilly. Colonel Kuznetsov had reported that." Hastings finished his coffee and set the cup on the table. "It might be to our mutual advantage if we were to work together to find Kuznetsov's assassin. What do we have to lose?"

"I can't do that."

"Why not?" He stared hard again. I didn't know whether this was the British stare or the Russian stare. Then he said, "Perhaps you did kill Kuznetsov. You were looking for Reilly; Kuznetsov got in the way; he threatened you; you had to kill him. Self-defense."

"It didn't happen."

"Then why won't you cooperate?"

"It doesn't work that way. I don't know who in the hell you are—except that it's pretty clear who you work for. And I'm not intimidated by that bulge under your jacket. I could kill you with my bare hands."

He raised his head and his eyebrows in a not-very-convincing expression of surprise. "Now, now. Calm yourself. Before we kill each other, we should conduct ourselves as gentlemen…If anyone were sitting nearby, they would surely find this an odd conversation."

My coffee was cold. I got up, walked over to the counter, poured out the cold, and refilled my cup. When I returned to the table, I said, "One of the reasons you believe me when I say I didn't kill your man is that I'm unarmed, and I'm always unarmed. You no doubt know that. If I'd confronted Kuznetsov, or if he had confronted me, I wouldn't have been able to shoot him. I have a gun, but I don't carry it."

"Forgive me for saying so, but that is negligent of you, Mr. Boudreau." He was back to Mister again. "It is almost professional malpractice."

"I'll try to do better in the future."

Hastings stood. "I'm going to grant you a reprieve today, but don't get in my way." He took a step away.

I said, "It's been a pleasure to meet you, Hastings. I'm sure our paths will cross again."

He paused, briefly. "Oh dear."

He left.

* * *

I made another call to Rabbit. "At a restaurant, I received a visit from one Ev Hastings. He walked up to my table and sat down."

"Holy damn! What in the hell is he doing there? The KGB must be taking this very seriously if Hastings is there."

"What do you know about him? Is he a heavyweight?"

Rabbit warned me, "Evelyn Hastings is very dangerous. I don't know that he's influential on KGB policy decisions, but he's a semi-famous operative. As you no doubt saw, he's English. He was trained originally by the Brits' Special Operations Executive during the war, a secret elite group specializing in sabotage and assassinations. He went over to the Russians years ago. After the war he doubled for a while, but he's now in the exclusive employ of the KGB. He's an assassin, or he has been—but he can do it all. I wonder whether we should send reinforcements. Do you need backup?"

"I don't think so. There was some bluster, but he knows I didn't kill Kuznetsov." I wanted to show Rabbit that I was on top of this. He likes self-confidence, and he doesn't like to have to reallocate manpower. "Hastings calls the man 'Colonel Kuznetsov', by the way."

"Yes, that was his KGB rank. It's good you met Hastings in a restaurant. That's safer than having him come to your room in the middle of the night."

I thought about that. "The restaurant is only a half-block from the city hall, but there isn't a big police presence on the street. He could've shot me in the restaurant and been long gone."

"Don't be too sure he wouldn't do that."

* * *

I don't know what Hastings was looking for in his questions, but I didn't give him the full story. The reason I was at Axton landing when I found the body is that I had seen, the day before, a small piece of paper posted on the bulletin board at the synagogue with the handwritten word "Axton." I thought it meant that the bad guys, or at least one of them, didn't know I was watching the bulletins. But it's likely Hastings—maybe only after the fact—knew I saw it, and he was testing me. Maybe he posted the Axton note there. Or maybe Kuznetsov did; or Reilly did; or the man who went to the Adirondack Hotel, "George Spelvin." This didn't get me very far. Those were all possibilities. And Spelvin might or might not have been Hastings with a phony accent. Using the name for a second role would suit his sense of humor.

I knew our side didn't post the Axton note, so it seemed likely that the opposition did it. How many men did the KGB have here? And, in addition to worrying about the KGB, I needed to find out who the young man was who ate fish with Kuznetsov at the Long Lake hotel. If I went to the hotel again, asking more questions, it would attract attention. The staff there would be curious, and that might start talk about the circumstances of Dr. Lien's death. We didn't want talk. It would also blow my cover. The KGB knew who I worked for but nobody else did, so far as I knew.

Speaking of blowing my cover, I thought maybe Linda needed to know what I was doing. It would make our relationship easier, more straightforward. And maybe she could help me identify the Russian's guest at the hotel fish fry. The waitresses in this area move around from one dining spot to another, part-time here and part-time there, and they often know each other. I thought Linda would be happy to ask some questions. There's always an apparent reason for an unmarried waitress to be interested in a young man. And I knew Linda had good sense. But the CIA wouldn't like it. They'd want to interview her ex-husband, her teachers, her landlord and former landlords, blah, blah, blah. I didn't want to subject her to that, and we didn't have time to wait for the clearance. You can't make an omelet without breaking the seal on the frozen food package.

* * *

When Linda got off work at the Full Moon, she went home to take care of her son, William. I stopped by with a bag of M&Ms for William. Linda doesn't approve of candy, but she's a softy and she decided to indulge both of us. After William went to bed, Linda and I talked. I jumped right into it. "In addition to being in the Air Force, I do some work for another government agency."

"What kind of work?"

I was partially responsive. "Information-gathering, investigations."

"Investigations of crimes?"

"Sometimes."

"Do you work for the FBI?"

"I can't tell you that. What I do is secret."

"Is it dangerous?"

"I hope not. Usually it's not, but it could be. Anyhow, I need help. Would you be willing to ask some questions? You couldn't tell people why you were doing it, but I don't think there'd be danger in this part of it."

Linda was cautious. "What would I be asking about? What's this all about?"

"Did you see the story in the *Adirondack Daily Enterprise* a week or so ago about a man who'd been found dead in the Raquette at Axton? I'm the guy who found him. The newspaper didn't say so, but he'd been shot."

"No, didn't see it. Who was he?"

"He was using the name 'Dr. Lien'."

"Do you mean that wasn't his real name?"

"Maybe not."

"If he wasn't using his real name and he was shot, this sounds dangerous to me."

That seemed like a reasonable proposition, but I tried to reassure her. "I don't think it's dangerous now. The bad guy is dead."

"Yeah, but who killed him?"

"I don't know. That's what I'm working on."

"What do you want me to do?"

"I'd like you to ask around at the Adirondack Hotel in Long Lake, probably asking people who worked the Friday fish fry in recent weeks. The manager of the hotel told me that the dead man, Dr. Lien, ate there at the fish fry with a younger man. I need to identify the younger man."

"Do you have any idea who he was?"

"Yeah. Just an idea. Do you know a guy named Bill Reilly—lives at Newcomb?"

"No, I don't think so. How old is he?"

"Late twenties. Works at the mine at Tahawus, in the offices, as a draftsman primarily."

"Don't know him. What are you looking for?"

"All I really want is whether he met with Dr. Lien at the hotel. I'll give you photographs of both Lien and Reilly, but it would be better if you didn't have to use them. Showing the photographs around makes it too much like police work."

"Yes, I can see that."

"It'd be better if you could just ask if they remember Lien having lunch with a younger man. And then you could ask what the younger man looked like. Of course it's possible they might know Reilly and say, 'Oh sure, Bill Reilly.' If that happens, you'll need to back off and pretend to be embarrassed, so they can assume it's a romantic interest. If they don't know him, a description will be enough."

"Okay, I think I can handle that. There's a girl who used to work at the Moon and is now a waitress at the hotel. I'm friendly with her. She lives in Saranac."

"Sounds good, only be sure not to tell her what it's about."

"I'll keep it casual."

"Thanks very much. You're a sweetheart."

"I hope so."

* * *

Two days later, Linda reported.

"It was pretty clearly Reilly. Betty doesn't know him, but her description of the guy fit perfectly. I didn't show her the pictures."

"That's good. A description will probably be enough."

Linda gave me the details—twenty-eight years old, five-eleven, slim, full head of light brown hair, blue eyes, light complexion, big nose. Betty didn't have quite all of that, but she had most of it and what she had described Reilly.

Then Linda said, "You may hear from Betty. She mentioned you. She said, 'I thought you were seeing Joe Boudreau.' At first

I told her, 'Oh please don't tell Joe.' Then, on second thought, I said, 'Oh go ahead and tell him. It might make him jealous.'"

I laughed. "Good thinking."

* * *

Another call to Rabbit. "I have a description of the younger man who met with Kuznetsov. It fits Bill Reilly. But I didn't want to wave Reilly's picture around—I thought that would attract attention we don't want."

"You're right about that. How sure are you that it was Reilly?"

"Pretty sure. I think if I confronted him with the facts, he'd probably break."

Rabbit was doubtful. "I don't think we have enough."

I pushed back. "I caught him in the act of passing microfilm to a Russian agent through a dead drop. What more do we need?"

"A map of mine tunnels and a bit of chemistry is a pretty long way from what the Pentagon is worried about. It appears that the KGB has some of the TFX specs. I'm not even sure that the security classification of the mine tunnels would hold up in a court. There may even be a survey filed somewhere."

"Only with restricted access, I think."

"Not good enough. And what about the murder? Do we want Reilly for that?"

I didn't think that made sense, and I said so. "Why would Reilly kill his Russian contact? Kuznetsov was probably paying him, or somebody Russian was, so why would he cut off that cash flow?"

Rabbit batted it back. "You tell me. That's why we need an

investigation. Maybe they argued about what Reilly was going to do, how far he'd go. Have you got a better candidate?"

"Maybe Hastings killed him, or George Spelvin, whoever that is. Hastings is an assassin. Maybe that's why he was sent here, to eliminate Kuznetsov. Why would any of them kill their own guy?"

Rabbit pursued it. "I'm betting on Reilly. He isn't a professional. He may be erratic, undisciplined. If Hastings did it, he'd have to have a very good reason. He'd need KGB approval."

"I'll continue to watch Reilly while Hastings watches me. But you aren't saying that I can't talk to Reilly, are you? That I can't confront him?"

"You'll have to use your own judgment about that. You're the man in the field. But you'll want to calculate how Hastings might react."

* * *

Newcomb, where Reilly lived, is just a short drive south of Tahawus, conveniently close to the mine. I'd already located Reilly's house, a small, old, frame bungalow in need of paint, like a dozen others in the town. The town didn't have many houses that weren't needing paint. But I decided that making an appointment to talk to him would be more businesslike and maybe more effective than just knocking on his door. He had a telephone. So I called him.

I said my name was Joe Boudreau. Why not? A good local name. But I just told him that I wanted to talk to him on business. I didn't give him any cover story; I didn't say what the business was. He was reluctant to agree to meet with me, so I offered to buy him lunch. I proposed that we go to the Friday fish fry at the Adirondack Hotel in Long Lake. As I intended, that shook him. He equivocated. Maybe he thought I was another Russian agent. Then there was a long pause. I wondered whether he was considering making a run for it. He might've been, but I suppose he decided to play out his hand and not panic. In any event, he agreed to meet me.

* * *

The dining room at the hotel was small, just a porch running across the front with windows overlooking the lake and two rows of tables. It didn't seat more than twenty-five or thirty. Two float planes, mounted on pontoons, tie up at a dock near the hotel. Diners occasionally see them take off or land. Tourists hire the planes for a hefty price to fly over the mountains and see whatever it is you see when you look down at the top of a mountain. Rock, I suppose. Or maybe God's handiwork. Preservationists try to keep the twentieth century from spoiling the quiet of the mountains, but modernity insists that we need machines.

I got to the hotel at ten minutes before twelve and Reilly was already there, waiting. He looked nervous. I chose to wear my uniform, but I was unarmed, as usual. I don't even know where a proper Air Force officer would wear a sidearm.

"Mr. Reilly, thank you for meeting with me."

"I didn't know you were in the Air Force."

"Well, as you see, I am."

"Is this Air Force business?"

I finessed the question. "We're developing a new airplane, a fighter. We call it the TFX, for 'tactical fighter experimental.' We're going to share it with the Navy. Maybe you've heard of it."

"Yes, I have."

"I'm told you like the fish fry here." He might have wondered how I knew that, but he didn't show it. "Want to have that?"

"Okay by me."

The waitress took our order. She wasn't Betty.

Then I continued the conversation. "I assume you know about the TFX because you work at the titanium mine."

"Yeah, maybe."

"So you know it will have titanium components."

"Yeah."

"How much more than that do you know?"

"Not much."

"You're not contributing a lot to this conversation, Bill. Since I'm buying you lunch, I need to get my money's worth. I'll bet you had more to say when you met here with Dr. Lien."

He didn't reply. I tried again.

"I don't want to ruin your appetite for the fish, so let's get this over with before the food arrives. I'm told you had lunch here, at the fish fry, with Dr. Lien."

Again, he didn't respond.

I repeated the name. "Dr. Lien." I paused. "Or perhaps you called him by a different name. I know Lien wasn't his real name."

"He told me he was Dr. Lien."

"What was your business with him?"

"He offered me a job."

"Doing what?"

"He said he was a mining engineer or a mining scientist, and he was interested in the mine at Tahawus."

"So what did he want from you?"

"Information."

"Information about what?"

"About the design of the mine."

"What about the airplane?"

"Airplane?"

"The TFX."

"We didn't talk about that."

"Uh, huh. But you didn't only talk. You also gave him some stuff, didn't you?"

"What d'ya mean? Like what?"

"Like microfilm."

"What?!" Reilly blanched.

The waitress arrived. "Here's your fish, gentlemen. I hope you enjoy your lunch. Could I get you anything else?"

I replied. "No, thanks, we're fine. We may not look like we're fine, but don't worry about us."

Then I said to Reilly, "So, where were we?"

He had figured it out. The waitress had given him a break. He said, "You were the guy at the cemetery, the bird watcher."

"That's right."

"I was worried about you."

"You should've been. You got caught, Mr. Reilly."

"What're you gonna do? Are you a cop, military police?"

"I'm asking the questions here." I ate fish and let him sit. Then, "Do you know what happened to Dr. Lien?"

"He's dead." Reilly said it quietly.

"How did he die?"

"I heard he was shot."

"The newspaper didn't say he was shot. How do you know that?"

"Somebody told me."

"Who?"

"A guy who worked with Lien." Reilly wasn't eating his fish. I was working on mine.

"What was his name?"

"I don't remember." He started to stand, but then sat down again and asked me, "Did you shoot Lien?"

"Did you?" I waited again. "Do you know what Lien's real name was?"

"Don't you know?"

"Yes," I said, "I know, but I want to find out whether you do."

"I think his name was Kuznetsov." There was no reason for him to answer me, but maybe he wanted to show that he was smart and well-informed.

"What kind of name is Kuznetsov?"

"I think it's Russian."

"Yeah, that's right. Why were you doing business with a Russian agent?"

"I don't have to answer that. I'm not going to say anything more until I talk to a lawyer."

"Okay, that's fine. But you might want to think about it. A lawyer probably couldn't help you with Hastings. Have you met Hastings yet?"

"Who's Hastings?"

"He's another Russian agent. He's British, but he's KGB. Kuznetsov was also KGB. If Hastings thinks you killed his partner, he'll be unhappy. Maybe even more unhappy than I am.... You haven't touched your fish."

Reilly's mouth was dry. He drank a whole glass of water. "I'm not hungry."

"Too bad. It's very good."

I decided to let him think about all this, and Linda and I

would watch to see what he did. I had a few more bites of fish, then paid the check and left. He was still at the table.

Chapter Four

Coreys, where Tiny Little has his place, is the settlement closest to Axton. I thought that maybe someone who lives there might know something about the murder, so I should talk to them, ask around. It was even possible that the killer lived there.

The only road to Axton passes through Coreys, three miles or so from the landing. If Kuznetsov and his murderer drove there, they went through the settlement. It was once a real village with a post office and a school. It has neither now, but older residents remember when it was a town and the name still appears on some maps, even new ones.

As you drive through the Adirondacks, you pass abandoned or semi-abandoned villages with small clusters of buildings, peeling paint, bad roofs, and broken windows. Some of these places were little more than logging camps—company towns that housed lumberjacks, field offices, and suppliers of basic provisions. But Coreys had a small hotel, some summer homes, and houses where guides lived when they weren't sleeping rough. Few of the houses there have been abandoned, most have been well-maintained, and investments have been made in improvements.

Coreys and Axton are near the center of a triangle formed by the villages of Long Lake, to the south, Tupper Lake, to the west, and Saranac Lake, to the east. Most of the towns here are named after lakes, so we usually just omit Lake from the name — the towns become Tupper or Saranac. But it doesn't work to just call a town Long. The book of large-scale maps of New York has the section with Axton on the cover, because it's interesting I suppose — mountains, lakes, the river. The landing is upstream of an oxbow in the Raquette, which is a riparian puzzle, as if the river loses its way. When you are canoeing through the oxbow, you have to look at the grasses in the water to determine which direction is downstream.

* * *

I went to the Hotel Saranac and found Ev Hastings in the lobby.

"Hello, Hastings, fancy meeting you here."

"I'd like to extend our conversation. Perhaps talking in your room would be better."

"I don't think so. I suggest we stand on the front steps of the City Hall and talk there."

"You are an amusing fellow, but if that is your preference, then by all means let us do that. Proceed."

We went out onto Temple Street and walked a block to the town offices, which are at a busy intersection. There's steady traffic and it would be difficult to escape from there quickly unless you had transportation waiting. Hastings probably thought I was a wimp to insist on meeting there, but at least I'd be a wimp who was alive. Besides, having him underestimate me was not such a bad thing.

I walked to the bottom of the City Hall steps, stood there, and asked, "What's on your mind?"

"I'm told that you met with Bill Reilly. Did you find it informative?"

"You knew I was watching him. It shouldn't surprise you that I talked to him. Unless you have agents or informants watching the fish fry constantly, which would be a strange use of manpower, I assume your information comes from Reilly himself. That's also not surprising. He's your guy."

"He *was* our guy. Or at least Kuznetsov's guy, but I don't think he is now. I think you recruited him, turned him."

I replied, "Why would I want him? He's a draftsman at the mine. The people I work for already have the specs. We don't need to get them from Reilly."

Hastings went on offense. "You want him to feed bogus data to us and to cover your tracks—your tracks in the killing of Kuznetsov."

I dismissed it. "Oh bullshit. You know better than that."

"You're still the only person we know of who was at Axton landing when, or near when, he was killed."

"You could've been there," I said. "I don't know that you weren't. Maybe you killed him. Maybe he went rogue. Maybe he went into business for himself. Maybe he decided that he liked America better than the gulag. So you killed him."

"Pretty flimsy, Joe. I know you didn't get any of that crap from Reilly. I've met with him, of course, but he isn't working for us now. He became worthless as soon as you knew about him. You'll be pleased to know that you frightened him. I frightened him too, I'm good at that. He's now about to wet his pants. I'm not entirely sure how that helps either one of us, but it's standard procedure. It's what the book prescribes." He paused. "Who killed Kuznetsov?"

"Maybe your man 'George Spelvin' did the job. How many agents do you have here? Or maybe you're George Spelvin."

Hastings laughed. "What an imagination! You should go to

Hollywood…I'm happy to give you Reilly. You're welcome to him. He's of no further use to us. I assume you'll want to prosecute him for espionage."

"If we did that, we'd subpoena you as a witness. Would you welcome that?"

"I'm afraid you'd find that I would be unavailable to testify."

"In the future, you'd have great trouble trying to reenter the United States."

"Come now. Don't be naïve. We both know there are ways."

An elderly woman walked up and stood nearby. I recognized her. She works at the public library, across the street from Hot Sara. I'm a customer or client of the library, or whatever it is we're called. I nodded to her and she nodded back. She said, "Hello, Captain."

I didn't know her name. I replied, "Good afternoon, pleasant day." She still stood there, so I said, "This is my British friend, Major Hastings." She didn't move, so I added some. "He constructs spy stories."

She was pleased. "Oh! Do you know John le Carre?"

Hastings said, somewhat obnoxiously I thought, "Yes, but I call him David. His name is David Cornwell, you know."

"I see. He must be interesting. He's a good writer."

Hastings smiled. "He is that."

As she left us, she said, "Peace be with you."

Hastings replied, "That is our prayer."

When she had gone, Hastings said, "You made me a Major."

"Compliments of the U. S. government."

"I should have thought Colonel, at the least. But you did have the grace to let me outrank you."

I replied, "Seniority, old chap."

Hastings turned toward the street. "Our conversations in

public are becoming a problem. Perhaps you might choose a place where you'd feel comfortable but where we would be less likely to be overheard."

"We could meet on a public beach, both wearing bathing suits. It's difficult to conceal a weapon in a bathing suit."

"I'm told that your technology division has solved that problem."

"Have you seen the product? It makes you appear to be in a constant state of arousal."

Hastings grimaced. "In some social situations, that would be awkward … In others, it might be welcomed."

"You're right. It's all a matter of timing."

Hastings said, "As with so many things." His eyes searched the street. Every pedestrian, every car that went by was entered into some file in his head. But he wasn't obvious about it. On the surface, he was nonchalant. He carried on the conversation, but "alert" doesn't begin to capture the degree of his awareness. I don't know whether he was looking for something in particular or this was just standard practice. The habit may be what has kept him alive. What a way to live. Is that what I want?

I tried to grasp a loose end. "There's one thing that puzzles me. Actually, there's more than one, but this thing especially puzzles me. Why did you use the name George Spelvin? We know where the name comes from — the theater convention. So were we supposed to recognize it? Was it some sort of signal? Did it mean that somebody was playing a double role? The obvious pseudonym had to be intentional."

"That was Vasily. He's an idiot. But we wanted you to know that we were paying attention, that we were operating here, not taking Kuznetsov's death lightly. We didn't want unintentional complications, collateral damage. So we wanted you to be on notice."

"Why didn't you just send a Hallmark card?"

"It's not our policy to announce that we have covert agents operating in your territory, but Vasily was clumsy. I was sent here to replace him."

"We are flattered."

* * *

Linda and I had a date that night. We went to the Cedar Grove in Tupper to avoid her friends at the Full Moon. Saranac is a small town, and a night out turns into an endless succession of greetings. People stop by your table, especially if you're in the military and haven't lived there for a few years.

We talked about how it happened that we both returned to the place where we grew up. I asked, "How did we end up in the Adirondacks?"

She spoke quietly. "I don't think we've ended up. I don't know about you, but I intend to keep going."

"So do I—so do I. But here we are, for now anyway. I know how I got here, the Air Force sent me." That was not the full story, as she knew by that time, but it was a safe way to talk in a restaurant. "But why did you return?"

"I was divorced. I had a son. My ex-husband was making child support payments, but I needed more money to provide a decent life for William. I needed a job. My parents were still in Saranac, and they were willing to help with childcare, which sure makes life easier. And I still have friends in the area—I thought the friends might provide contacts who could help me find a job. Besides, Saranac is a nice town. It's a good place for a child to grow up."

"Those are all good reasons. I've thought about moving back, but if I stay in my job they'll send me God-knows-where. It's not a good career for somebody who wants to settle down."

"Do you want to settle down?" She stopped short. "Oh, damn! I'm sorry. That came out sounding like something different than what I intended. What I meant was, are you thinking about changing jobs?"

"Don't worry about the question. The short version of the answer is that I've thought about a change, but I don't really know what else I'd do. What I'm doing now is what I was trained for. It's pretty specialized. I suppose I could try to be a private investigator, but most of that is really boring. Mostly what they do is take pictures of husbands and wives, usually husbands I think, in bed with people they're not married to. That might be amusing the first time or two, but it doesn't seem like a worthwhile way to spend your life. And it could be more dangerous than what I'm doing now…But I've thought about settling down."

"I'm not asking for a commitment, you understand."

"I understand. It's too early for that. But it's always interesting to know what's going on—what the other guy, or girl, is thinking."

"Yes, it is." She paused again, and toyed with her barbecued ribs. "If you wanted to do less traveling, less moving around, would you consider coming back here?"

"Sure. Saranac would be near the top of my list. Just after Paris." I intended that to be a joke. I'm not sure it came out that way. Why should mature adults on a date be so damned awkward? Still walking on eggshells. "If I was looking for a permanent home, Saranac is the most likely place. I like the town.

It's beautiful—cold, but beautiful. There are lots of Boudreaus. That's mostly a plus." I paused and took a deep breath. "And, most important, Linda Coyle is in Saranac. I like you Linda, I really like you. I'm being careful—maybe I should put it more strongly than that."

"I really like you, too, Joe. I always have—even in high school."

After dinner, we started to drive back to Saranac, but we got only a mile or so before I turned off on a side road. As it happened, we were near the Jewish cemetery with the dead letter box. Just beyond it there's a sand pit where high-quality fill is excavated for construction projects. The road was deserted at that time of night. I pulled over and stopped. We kissed. Then we kissed some more. We both knew where it was going. I unfastened her bra. She put her hand on my upper thigh. Then a little higher. I unzipped her pants. It just sort of happened. At that point, we decided, mutually, that it would be better to find a more private place. There was a babysitter at her house, so my hotel room was the obvious choice.

She said, "If we go up in the elevator together, there'll be talk."

"Do you care?"

"Not really."

"Good."

* * *

Rabbit sent me an encrypted telex with some additional information about Bill Reilly that the Agency had acquired from a recent graduate of SUNY Albany. The informant, who'd been active in SDS at Albany at the same time as Reilly, was charged with possession and distribution of marijuana and he wanted that charge to go away. I suspect it was a large quantity of marijuana. In any event, the report was that Reilly was a loner, had no friends, always needed money, and had a bad relationship with his parents. Or no relationship — they had disowned him or he had disowned them. Either way, he didn't have a refuge. He was the sort of guy who was made to order as an asset for Kuznetsov.

The picture Rabbit had pieced together suggested that Kuznetsov, probably in his Dr. Heinrich Lien role, had befriended Reilly, cultivated him. It wasn't clear about whether Reilly was already at the mine before Kuznetsov focused on him or whether Reilly was recruited by the Soviets before he got the job at the mine and the KGB was then involved in placing him there. So we don't know how long the operation had been in progress, but it wasn't a recent thing. There had been some investment.

Why they did it also wasn't clear. Linda and I discussed this. It seemed that the Russians wanted scientific data from the Tahawus lab, but where did the TFX design specs come from? The mine didn't have much to do with the airplane, and why were they interested in a map of the tunnels? What were the tunnels used for?

Linda told me she'd read about an iron mine at Tahawus that preceded the titanium mine. She hadn't intended to have a career as a waitress, so she studied library science at SUNY Canton with a specialty in archival work, and she'd long had an interest in local history. The old mine had operated for thirty years in the middle of the nineteenth century, and it had a blast furnace and a forge, brick kilns, and other buildings. The blast furnace was still standing. The mine had gone out of business because there was some contaminant in the iron ore. The contaminant was later found to be titanium.

Linda thought there had to be some reason why the KGB wanted the map of the tunnels—the map that Reilly had microfilmed and given to Kuznetsov. She insisted, "There's something important or useful about the layout of those tunnels." She knew that St. Lawrence University at Canton held archives concerning the economic history of the region. Might there be a map of the iron mine? She volunteered to check it out.

To get from Saranac Lake to Canton, you drive north, almost to the St. Lawrence River, almost to Canada. On the way, you leave the Adirondack Park, a huge tract administered by the State of New York but with a lot of private land within it. For some reason that isn't clear to me, the boundary of the park is called the "Blue Line." After you cross it, the road descends from the mountains and enters relatively flat pastureland with grazing animals and grain fields. Some old dairy barns still stand, but most of the dairies have moved elsewhere. Where did they go? Why would they want to leave the St. Lawrence valley, a lovely, gentle place? Maybe there wasn't good enough transportation to get the dairy products to urban centers. We all need to live on top of each other.

"Special Collections" is on the second floor of the old library, one of the university's first buildings. That's where they keep pre-Columbian pots and the drawings, papers, and books of John Henry Rushton, the great Canton canoe builder of the nineteenth century. But the archives are in the basement, in dense storage. The archives office has a couple of windows opening into a light well located in a sort of moat around the building. There are two tables and several chairs, but the documents themselves are in space that is temperature and humidity controlled. Library staff fetch them upon request. So Linda searched the catalogue and located a set of papers labeled "Tahawus Mine".

There were three 9x12 archival boxes, with lids. She went through all three. The first two had business papers—contracts made by the various companies that owned the mine, copies of deeds, bills of sale, the incorporation papers of a private hunting and fishing club that owned the property in the late nineteenth and early twentieth centuries, and other documents. The design drawings for the blast furnace were there. The third box had maps, one with the buildings at the modern titanium mine, except for the laboratory; another with the location of the old iron mine and of the village built to house the workers; and one with the layout of the office and workshop buildings at the iron mine, and an attachment showing the location of the tunnels. It wasn't clear how much of the tunneling was actually done before the company went bankrupt.

It looked to me like the pit for the modern mine penetrated or destroyed some of the old tunnels, but not most of them. If all of the planned tunnels were built, the inside of that mountain must look like a piece of Swiss cheese. Do the Soviets want to use the tunnels to access the mine, perhaps especially the laboratory? The property is protected by guards around-the-clock, but maybe the tunnels provide a way to get behind the guards. The manager of the mine should know the answer to that question. Or was something stored in the tunnels? Something the enemy might want? I could ask about that too, but I wasn't sure that the present management would know the answer. They didn't care about the iron mine. Had Kuznetsov discovered an angle we didn't know about? I thought there had to be a secret here somewhere.

Linda asked when those files were last accessed. The library's records showed that the Tahawus material had been requested thirteen months before, but the name of the requesting party was missing. It was, of course, possible that Kuznetsov or one of his buddies was doing some research. It was also possible that a student was writing a term paper.

* * *

Then Hastings approached me again about cooperating to investigate Reilly. Of course I'm always cautious about the motives of the KGB, so I decided to consult Rabbit and seek his advice. He had a lot more experience in this work. He called the shots, and I respected his judgment.

I asked him whether I should meet with Hastings. His immediate reaction was that he didn't see any harm in it so long as I wasn't concerned about my personal safety. I said I didn't think Hastings had anything to gain by harming me, which would bring the Agency down on him, hard. But I also thought that the KGB might have eliminated Kuznetsov for reasons of its own. Maybe Vasily, the man who called himself Spelvin, shot him—maybe that's why Vasily was pulled out of the field. And, by the way, where was Vasily now? Did we know what had become of him? Maybe he also was dead.

Rabbit said, "I don't think the KGB killed Kuznetsov. If they'd done it, they would've been less obvious about it. He would've drowned. He wouldn't have a bullet in his head—unless, of course, they didn't have any choice because he was about to shoot them."

I said, "That seems to me to be less than a sure thing."

"There's a lot of uncertainty in this business."

"Yeah."

"If you wanted certainty, you should've invested in railroads."

So I told Hastings that I'd meet him for dinner at Little Italy in Tupper. As on the dinner date with Linda, I wanted to get out of Saranac in order to avoid attention. And thinking of Linda, it occurred to me that she might like to go with me so that she would have the full story. I knew it would be a help to have her there. She has a good head on her shoulders, and she'd provide another set of ears to hear Hastings and assess what he was up to. But I decided not to tell him in advance that Linda would be there. It could be a surprise — keep him off balance.

So I walked into the restaurant with Linda and introduced her to Hastings. He was at a booth in the back.

I said, "Linda is my friend and she's helping me on this."

Hastings nodded. "I see. She's rather like me then."

Linda and I laughed. Linda said, "Well, perhaps just a bit different."

When I introduced him to Linda, I again called him "Major Hastings." He picked up on it.

"Major! Here I am, fifty years old and still a major. Sometime soon I should be promoted."

I replied. "I'll put in a good word."

We ordered promptly. Hastings told the waitress, "Spaghetti with nothing but melted butter — real butter, no oleomargarine. And a large glass of Montepulciano, please."

I said, "Butter will clog up your arteries."

"Ahh. Thank you for your touching concern, but note what I have with it. Cheap red wine contains tiny scrub brushes, microscopic brushes that scour the arteries. Butter on spaghetti is flavorful and, when combined with the Montepulciano, results in the splendid specimen of manhood you see before you."

"I've heard that before."

"Oh, are the scrub brushes well-known in the States?"

"They are."

"Why, then, are you not drinking red wine?"

"Employees of my company don't drink on duty."

"Pity. Yet another reason to be on the other side." He un-rolled his napkin and rearranged his silverware to suit him. "And is going out to dinner with your girlfriend one of your duties?"

I said, "That depends. If somebody at the dinner is carrying a Webley, I'm on duty."

"Oh, the Webley is only for daytime. I have my evening arsenal tonight."

"And what is that?"

"Not to worry, old boy." He turned to Linda. "But we must be boring you, my dear."

Hastings stood. He took from a side pocket of his suitcoat a silk handkerchief in a paisley pattern, blue and red and yellow, neatly folded into a square. He held one edge between his thumb and forefinger and shook it casually to get rid of the folds. Then he stuffed the handkerchief into the breast pocket of his jacket so that half was sticking out, just odd bits and pieces. He left it that way. It was quite a performance. If we wanted to be inconspicuous, this wasn't the way to do it. Not many of Little Italy's customers wear ties or suits, much less silk handkerchiefs. He didn't give a damn.

I think the display was intended to amuse Linda. It did. Or maybe it was the old magician's trick—distract the eye, move the eye to the left while inserting a rabbit into a hat on the right. Or maybe he just wanted to annoy me. He accomplished that too.

So I said, "Now that that's taken care of, what's on the agenda?"

"Cooperation, my boy, cooperation. The world needs more of it."

"No doubt. But I don't think we're after the same thing, or have the same goals."

"Of course we do. We both want to find the person who killed Colonel Kuznetsov, surely."

"The last I heard, you thought I did that."

"Oh, that was just a passing fancy of my superiors. I don't think it ever really troubled you."

I still didn't think cooperation made sense. "For all I know, you killed him."

Once again, he turned toward Linda. "You really must work on improving Joe's manners. I'm sure you feel that that's not a polite way to talk to a dinner companion."

She replied, "Mr. Hastings, you treat this investigation as if it is all a big joke. Joe and I are serious about this, even if you are not."

"Well." He took two generous swallows of wine. "It is, of course, all a performance, my dear. In my line of work, I have a limited range of options, a limited number of roles. One is the rather clownish, rather fey buffoon you have seen." His smile went away. The hard look appeared. "I could be more stern. I don't think you would like it." He relaxed again. "Young women, too, I believe, have a choice among roles. Some are more socially acceptable, more charming than others." He smiled. "You are performing yours very well. My congratulations."

Our food arrived and Hastings refilled his wine glass from the carafe. He toyed with his spaghetti. He appeared to be more interested in talking than eating. He said, "How much do you know about Reilly's background with us?"

I didn't know much, so I said, "What do you mean?"

"Well, if we're going to solve the killing of Kuznetsov, I'll probably have to trust you a bit, and since Reilly is no longer of use to us in any case, now that you are on to him, I'll tell you that we've been in contact with him for some time."

"Is, or was, Reilly on your payroll?"

"He never was, or not much, just small amounts to cover some travel expenses. He's not an entrepreneur. Reilly is a true believer."

"How long has he been in touch with you?"

"I'm not at liberty to be very specific."

"Has he given you valuable material?"

"I can't discuss that. I've given you as much as you need to know. As a gesture of mutual friendship."

"What do we do now?"

Hastings said, "Squeeze him, I suppose. I would think that you already have enough to prosecute. You could certainly threaten him."

"Would you testify?"

"No. Of course not. I can't do that."

"Yes, okay. I suppose the Justice Department could make the case without you."

"You certainly could if Langley wanted it done. Your agents inside Russia would help." He smiled.

"We might have to give up someone in order to do that."

"Yes, perhaps. It's a question of whether you want to catch Kuznetsov's killer. You may have to pay a price for that."

I asked, "But how much does Reilly know? Do you think he did it? Why would he?"

"I don't know. But Reilly was in contact with Kuznetsov. We both know that. He was there, on the scene. He had the opportunity. Did he have the motive? That remains to be seen."

* * *

I reported to Rabbit as usual. I recall his reaction vividly. "*Cooperation* with Hastings! You have got to be kidding."

"Well, Rabbit, his man was killed on our turf. We should probably try to catch the killer."

"I've told you before that Hastings is a killer. He may well have done the job."

"I don't think so."

"You don't think so." There was something in his voice. It may have been caution or it may have been disappointment. "He probably wants you to 'cooperate' so that he can keep you close, so he can see whether you're on his trail."

"That occurred to me. I won't give him sensitive information. He's already told me that Reilly worked for them for some time. So I've already received something useful, or maybe useful, from him. Surely we don't want an all-out war between our intelligence services."

"Joe, Hastings is the enemy. Intelligence services are always at war. There's no ceasefire. This doesn't smell right. He's up to something. We have to figure out what it is."

"Yeah, that makes sense."

"Okay, you can listen to Hastings, but don't talk."

Chapter Five

There were then a couple of weeks during which I dealt with Hastings and Rabbit and attempted to balance the two of them. Strategizing. But there was a distraction — Linda got a new job opportunity, and she welcomed it. As is often the case with job openings in the Adirondacks, however, it came about because of someone else's misfortune. A teacher of American history at the high school retired suddenly as a result of an emergency appendectomy with a bad outcome, and Linda's reputation as a local historian came to the mind of the school's principal. Linda didn't wish the poor teacher ill health, but she was glad to stop taking orders for two eggs scrambled with bacon, hold the toast.

She knew most of the other teachers at the school, and the students were often fun (sometimes not), but the parents were a pain. They wanted their kids to learn things, or at least be able to get a job, but they didn't want demands made on them that would interfere with football or duck hunting or household chores. You were supposed to motivate students without bothering them. The best way to do that, of course, was to teach things that were interesting. Interesting material, however, carried its own risks.

After a month at the school, Linda taught a "unit" (something like two or three classes) on Lord Jeffrey Amherst and the Indians. The problem was that Lord Jeff stood accused of giving blankets infected with smallpox to the troublesome natives, and the allegation was that this was intentional, an early form of biological warfare. Now, the fact that Linda's class was discussing this came to the attention of a local banker, one McKenzie Denleigh, known as "Mac." Mac is a patriot. He went to Williams, not Amherst, mind you, but he is broadminded and always willing to defend the wrongly accused. Or even, perhaps, on occasion, the rightly accused. He is, indeed, also willing to accuse. He complained about Linda. He delivered his complaint to the high school principal at the Saranac Shores Country Club, and the complaint came with more heat than did the chicken a la king. The principal was made uncomfortable, and the principal soon passed that discomfort along to Linda.

It was not entirely clear how Mac's enthusiastic support of Lord Amherst fit the patriotism theme, given that Amherst was a British general, but never mind. Mac said Amherst was innocent. And it turned out that there was, in fact, some disagreement among scholars about the extent of Amherst's complicity. Here is the story: In the French and Indian War, Amherst commanded the British army in North America. During the Indian assault on Fort Pitt (now Pittsburg) in 1763, he wrote to one of his colonels suggesting that blankets infected with smallpox be sent to the Indians in order "to extirpate this execrable race," but it isn't clear that the colonel acted on the suggestion. There is reasonably clear documentation that unwashed blankets taken from the smallpox hospital were given to a delegation of Indians as a gift, but there isn't evidence that it was done as a result of Amherst's letter or that Amherst even knew about it. The gift of the blankets, very likely intended to infect, was approved by another British general, Thomas Gage, not Amherst. Now, from a patriotism standpoint or any other, I didn't see why the complicity of General Gage was better than Amherst's, but again never mind. Mac Denleigh was clear that Linda's classes had been a slur upon the honor of …someone.

The argument among historians about how to interpret the evidence might well have provided the basis for good classroom discussion or debate, but before any such thing could happen, Denleigh had organized his troops. The principal received more complaints and Linda's job was threatened. So was her reputation in the community. Her parents were upset. I needed to defend her.

I was not without resources. Langley has a first-rate research department and amazing files. I asked one of my friends from spook school what they had, if anything, on McKenzie Denleigh. Mac is clearly a jackass, which is widely recognized, but he is also clearly of the local blowhard variety, so I wasn't expecting much.

The answer that came back was that the file on Mac was thin, but it turned out that he had a son, Hudson Denleigh, known as "Hud," who had an interesting profile. Hud was a pain-in-the-ass of a different type. He had gone to the All Saints School (a name notable for its inclusiveness), which was a finishing school for boys, and then on to the University of Virginia, where he was presently enjoying himself. While in school, probably at All Saints, he became persuaded by the views of Herbert Marcuse, a Marxist scholar and the leading theorist of the New Left. One of Hud's teachers recruited him for the revolution.

But Hud was conflicted at best. His clothes came from what he called "the brothers Brooks," and he sandpapered the collars and cuffs of his Oxford cloth button-downs to create the appearance that he had grown up with them. On the other hand, he joined the campus chapter of the Progressive Labor Party, a Communist-front group. This put him on my turf. CIA was supposed to monitor the threat from the Left (although, admittedly, the motivation in this case was a bit more personal).

So I made an appointment to see Hud's old man. He wasn't very busy, which surprised me. Do the presidents of small banks have a lot of spare time? I didn't even have to tell his secretary why I wanted to see him, but maybe the "Captain Boudreau" got me in the door. A large photograph of General Douglas MacArthur hung on the wall in Denleigh's office. I resisted the impulse to salute it. Why MacArthur? Maybe the McKenzie and MacArthur clans shared a castle, or a distillery.

Denleigh hauled himself out of his swivel chair and shook my hand. "What may I do for you, Captain?"

I was polite. "Thank you for seeing me. I'm here because I hope we can resolve the misunderstanding about Linda Coyle's history class at the high school."

There were two chairs in front of the desk, but he moved back behind it and sat down. He didn't invite me to sit, but I did. He replied, "I don't think there's any misunderstanding. She taught that Lord Jeffrey Amherst gave the Indians blankets infected with smallpox. That's a scurrilous story that's never been proven. Why not teach something positive about American history?"

"Well, just to clarify, I don't think anyone suggested that Lord Jeff delivered the blankets personally. The question is whether he gave the order that it be done. There's some disagreement among historians about how to interpret the evidence on that."

"Well, if there's disagreement about it, why teach it? Why not stick to settled facts so you know what you're talking about? Not just scurrilous speculation or horror stories."

"There's still in existence a document, a letter in Amherst's handwriting addressed to Major Bouquet, one of his subordinates." I pulled a sheet of paper from my jacket pocket. "Amherst says, 'Could it not be contrived to send the Small Pox among those disaffected tribes of Indians?'"

Denleigh's voice came from down near his shoes. "How do we know that's not a forgery?"

I took that as desperation, so I let it pass. I said, "Linda thought the controversy about what Lord Amherst did or didn't do would be a good lesson for her students. It shows the kinds of evidence used by historians, and how the evidence can be interpreted differently, so that even experts disagree about what happened. Not everything is certain."

He said, "Linda Coyle should teach what we know, not what we don't know. Not just speculation. And she should teach the great American story, not a pack of lies. Education should be inspiring—it shouldn't discourage the students. It should send them out into the world with enthusiasm, and with pride in this great country. Why not tell them about General Washington?"

It occurred to me to ask whether she should teach them that Washington owned slaves, but I held my tongue, mostly, sort of. I said, "I'm a military officer, Mr. Denleigh. I've heard a great many Fourth of July speeches. I'm serving my country, but I don't know that hearing those speeches has made me a better officer."

Denleigh's face turned red. He hadn't served in the military. I knew that.

Now he was obviously angry. "Linda Coyle should not be teaching. She isn't qualified. She doesn't have the right values."

The fat was in the fire. I shot back. "You have a son, Mr. Denleigh. He's at the University of Virginia I believe."

"Yes, indeed. Hudson is a fine boy, and UVA is Mr. Jefferson's school, you know."

"And do you speak to Hudson—you call him 'Hud,' I believe—do you speak to him often?"

"Of course I do. Often enough."

"And are you aware of the organizations and activities in which Hud participates?"

"His fraternity, do you mean?"

"I had in mind his political affiliations."

He blanched. I think he knew the story. But he put on a brave face. "What do you mean?"

"I'm informed that Hud is active in the Progressive Labor Party, a Marxist organization, essentially a front for the Community Party."

Denleigh jumped to his feet. "What gave you that idea?"

"I have access to confidential information. I assure you that it's accurate. You might want to speak to Hud about it, but I think you already know that what I'm saying is true."

Denleigh walked to the window and looked out over downtown Saranac. The bank was not a tall building. We were on the third floor, the top floor. He looked at the dark clouds and said, "It looks like rain."

I replied, "We don't need that."

But he wasn't ready to give up. Maybe his view of the town had given him confidence. He thought he owned the place. He held up his left hand, casually pointed out the window with his index finger, and nodded. I think he meant that I was supposed to come to the window and look out. But I didn't. I stayed seated. So he went on. "One of the advantages of a small town, Captain, is that it's manageable." He brushed a small piece of lint off the sleeve of his suit coat. "Of course you have to know how to manage it. The people of the town have to understand the rules. They learn what they can get away with and what they cannot. If they violate the rules, they're punished. That keeps things orderly, which is the way most people like it. It's the way I like it."

"I grew up here, Mr. Denleigh. I understand this town." He was still standing, but I just looked at him and spoke calmly. "You are going to drop this silly campaign about Lord Jeffrey Amherst, and Linda Coyle is going to keep her job. Otherwise the people of this town will hear about Hud Denleigh's political activity. They'll hear that the son of the president of their bank is a communist. The golfers at the Saranac Shores Club won't like it."

"You are misusing government information."

"That may be so, but that won't help you."

"It is a dirty business."

"Yes, it is."

His face was red. He paced the floor as he spoke. "You will not say anything about my son, Mr. Boudreau. Hear me now. You have uncles and cousins in this area. Hear me. Your uncles and cousins have loans from my bank. They're dependent on those loans for the operating capital of their businesses and, in many cases, for the mortgages on their homes. Hear me now. The loan contracts have provisions that permit me to call the loan, to demand repayment, and if you say anything about this, I'll require payment in full. Your uncles and cousins will lose their businesses. They'll go bankrupt. Many of them will lose their homes. Hear me."

"You won't do that."

"Why not?"

"Because, if you do, the people of this town will take their money out of your bank. The Boudreaus have been in Saranac for a long time and have many friends. The people here like the Boudreaus, and they don't much like the Denleighs. You lord it over them. People know that the Boudreaus are just like them. If you hurt the Boudreaus, the people will punish you. You have much more to lose than I do, or my family. When the town found out what was going on, they'd see that the management of this bank can't be trusted, that it's unreliable. There'd be a run on the bank. You'd be finished in this town. Done, permanently."

Mac Denleigh said, "What?"

I replied, "You're done."

Denleigh was silent. I thought he was going to cry. He was used to giving commands, not receiving them. I think he was more frightened that I had the guts to say these things than he was by the substance of my threat. This upended his world. If people stopped being afraid of him, stopped obeying his orders, that would destroy the structure of his life.

He sat down. He was silent again, longer this time. Then, "I'll be quiet. Linda Coyle can teach whatever damn thing she wants."

I made it specific. "You'll tell the high school principal that you've looked into it and thought it over, and you're going to drop the matter. Tell him that you'll let him run the high school."

"Yes, I'll do that."

"And I'll still have a copy of Hud's file."

"You are a son of a bitch."

"I'm a warrior." I hoped he couldn't see how little I believed that.

* * *

I met Linda at the high school at the end of the day and greeted her with the news. "I met with Mac Denleigh. I don't think you'll have any more trouble from him."

"How did you do that?"

"I reasoned with him. I appealed to his better nature. He saw the merit of my arguments."

She almost smiled, but not quite. "You didn't hit him, did you?"

"No. I did not."

"This job means a lot to me, Joe. And to William. I'm very grateful."

I was pleased about that, of course, but I remembered Denleigh saying that it was a dirty business. I agreed with him.

* * *

Linda and I had to hunt for Reilly. He'd bolted. For all I knew, he was in Russia. I couldn't find anyone who had seen him recently, or anybody who would admit to it. Linda checked with her waitress friends but didn't turn up any leads. Reilly's house in Newcomb was still furnished. I could see through the windows that his furniture and TV set were there. The neighbors hadn't seen him for "a while."

East of Newcomb, there's a road that goes north to the mine and to an old village called Adirondac. Miners once lived there, but now it's just a small cluster of abandoned houses. Broken windows, missing doors. Scavengers have been there to get parts. The roofs are starting to go.

Linda said to me, "Let's check out Adirondac. Reilly needs shelter and he might be able to find it there. You don't sleep out in the woods here without shelter."

That made sense to me. "Good idea. He works at the mine,

or he did, so he knows that area. Maybe one of the old houses has a dry place for a sleeping bag."

We drove up the mine road. A railroad track runs along much of it. In the 19th century, there was a smelter at the mine site, and the trains carried pig iron instead of ore. There's also a river that winds beside the road — it's either the Opalescent River or the North Branch of the Hudson, I'm never sure which — and the road crosses the river several times. The woods are so thick there that you don't get many views of either the tracks or the river from the road, but you hear the water rushing down the hill. You can tell the road is climbing — you have to shift down. There are some switchbacks. There's a considerable change in elevation between Newcomb and the mine.

We parked near the mine. A trail runs north from there through the Indian Pass to Lake Placid, and hikers have cleared a few parking spaces. Linda and I went straight to the dilapidated houses. Rain overnight had made the path muddy, and there were no new footprints in the mud, but we could still see old prints leading from the road toward one of the houses. That didn't mean much — hikers on their way to Indian Pass often see the old houses and then decide to check them out.

The door to the first house was open, not wide open but ajar by six inches or so. Rain had blown in. The place was cheaply built and falling apart, but the partitions were still there. The room the door opened into was probably the living room. It was small, but had a window. An even smaller room beside it may have been the bedroom, and one on the back with a sink must have been the kitchen. Those smaller rooms also had windows — one each. Three rooms, three windows, not one of which wasn't broken. No bathroom.

I looked for bullet holes, but didn't see any. Linda found a worn-out pair of men's work boots, the soles separating from the uppers. They hadn't been worn recently. There was space on the floor where someone could have unrolled a sleeping bag, if they were really desperate, but there was no evidence that anybody had done so.

Linda and I explored the six remaining houses with similar results—no real sign of Reilly. We had known it was a long shot. Investigative work is like that—lots of blind alleys and dead ends. It's a wonder that Dashiell Hammet and Raymond Chandler could make books out of it.

When we finished exploring the mine's old houses, we drove back to Saranac <u>via</u> Long Lake and stopped at the hotel for something to eat. I greeted the desk clerk there and she told me that "Mr. Spelvin" had returned. She seemed flustered. She said that, when she mentioned to him that Captain Boudreau had inquired about Dr. Lien, Spelvin was uncommonly interested and asked her how he could get in touch with me. She gave him the contact information I had left with her—she hoped that was all right. What I had given her was the phone number and address of the Hotel Saranac. So Spelvin, the Soviet agent Hastings called Vasily Rostov, now knew that I was working on the case, and he knew where to find me. That wasn't good. Of course Hastings could have given him the same information, but I didn't think he would have. Hastings didn't like Rostov. Professional jealousy or competition for favor from Moscow might have been a part of it, but, as I found out, Rostov was not very likeable. I didn't find him charming.

When I got back to Hot Sara, there was a message that Mr. Spelvin had called and that he wanted to meet with me. I had other plans. Apart from concern about my personal safety, and Linda's, I was trying to track Reilly and I didn't want Spelvin/

Rostov to get in the way. Why was he sent here? Why wasn't Hastings sufficient? What were the Soviets concerned about in the northern Adirondacks?

I didn't return Rostov's call, but I did contact Hastings. He'd taken a house as a short-term rental. I don't know how long he planned to stay.

"Colonel Hastings, it's the captain here."

"Ah, you're feeling playful today. I'm finally promoted. That's a good sign. Is there good news?"

"No, I don't think so, but there is news. I've been told that George Spelvin has returned."

"Yes, indeed he has. In fact, he's here with me now."

"Oh, okay, why has he come back?"

"I don't know. I'll ask him … Vasily, why in the hell are you here?"

There was the sound of a door, closing. Hastings said, "He appears to have gone out."

Hastings didn't offer any further comment on that, so I said, "There was a message waiting for me at the hotel. I was told he wanted to talk."

Hastings said, "He may be on his way there now. Be careful."

"What do you advise?"

"Be prepared — always good advice. The Boy Scout motto, I believe."

"You're up on all the American lore."

"The Scouts were founded by Lord Baden-Powell, dear boy. We knew him as the Baron Gilwell."

"Thank you for that."

"Seriously, now, you want to be armed." Hastings was through with banter.

"Why? What's up?"

"Vasily claims to believe that you killed Kuznetsov. I've told him that that's rot, but he insists. He's rather an idiot, I'm afraid."

"Why would I have killed Kuznetsov instead of using the usual channels for getting foreign agents out of the country?"

"Pique, I suppose. Vasily may be doing this for reasons of his own, or maybe he has a superior who wants you gone. The Kremlin knows many things. Perhaps you have a past that's unknown to me."

"Yeah, and unknown to me too."

He said, "Just watch out. Vasily is dangerous. An idiot, but a dangerous idiot."

I left the hotel and walked down the street to the Full Moon. If Rostov was going to show up, I didn't want to be alone in my room with no one around. I wanted company. I told the hotel's desk man where I was going.

It was the middle of the afternoon and the restaurant was quiet. There were a few people sitting at tables reading newspapers and nursing cups of coffee. I was one of them. The owner of the Moon, Pierre Fortune, stopped by my table and I invited him to join me. I knew him from the old days—when I was in high school he had another place. Pierre's an old bobsledder, what we call a "slider." He competed until his legs gave out. He's a large man and he provided some weight on the sled. He'd provide more now. An apron was wrapped around him and it displayed some of the day's offerings. Pierre is a good cook.

As I was talking to him, a man arrived at the front door—a very big man, even bigger than Pierre. He entered and stood by the door. His eyes went immediately to me—he certainly recognized me, probably from a picture. He stared. I'd never seen him before, but he fit the description in the Agency's files. Pierre noticed the two of us looking at each other and said, "Do you know that guy?"

I replied, "Not really, but I know who he is."

"Who?"

"A bad guy. A Russian."

Vasily Rostov was six feet three inches tall and maybe 230 pounds with not a lot of flab. Not quite an NFL lineman, but close. He had thick black hair, heavy eyebrows, and a prominent jaw. I wasn't close enough to see the color of his eyes. You could cast him as Frankenstein's monster and not have to use much makeup.

Pierre stood, said, "I don't especially like Russians," and walked over toward Rostov. The two of them talked, very briefly. I couldn't hear them from where I was sitting. Then the Russian left without saying anything to me.

Pierre returned to my table and said, "What was that?"

I held my palms up. "Damned if I know."

Pierre didn't believe me, but didn't pursue it. He said, "I told him that if he didn't want to order anything he should leave. He looks like a weightlifter." He wiped his hands on his apron and walked back to the kitchen.

* * *

I reported to Rabbit by telephone. When I had finished, he asked the obvious question:

"What in the hell is going on there? Suddenly Saranac Lake is a popular destination for Soviet agents. First Kuznetsov, then Hastings, now Vasily Rostov. The KGB must have a special on downhill skiing. I still can't figure out why Ev Hastings is there. Either someone high up really cares about this operation, or they want us to think someone high up really cares. Unfortunately, we don't know which of those plausible hypotheses is the accurate one." Rabbit cleared his throat. He may just have been gathering his thoughts. "Why should the Soviets attach so much importance to the murder of one nickel-dime agent? Field agents are killed all the time—and I don't say that just to worry you. Kuznetsov had been around for years without attracting much attention. He was an everyday operative. So what's the big deal? What is it that they really care about?"

I reviewed the facts. "Well, we know Kuznetsov wanted data from the mine, or at least that's what Reilly passed to him, including a map of the tunnels. So we know it has something to do with the mine. And the killing took place at Axton landing or the body floated there from somewhere nearby, and that's pretty close to the mine. And now Reilly has disappeared. We probably should have arrested him when we had the chance."

Rabbit defended his strategy. "We wanted him to lead us to more evidence, and that may be working. Rostov is probably here because Reilly is still at large and they want to get hold of him before we do. He knows things. Reilly is certainly the key to this, or at least he's the best key we have. We can't let them take him off the board.... You're outnumbered now—should I send reinforcements?"

I knew that Linda would help me, but I didn't think it would be advisable to tell Rabbit that, so I just said, "I don't know what reinforcements could do that I'm not doing now. The Adirondacks is a big place; we can't look behind every tree. And Ev Hastings keeps saying that we should cooperate on this."

Rabbit was alarmed. "Don't take that bait. It's a trap. I don't know what game they're playing, but Hastings is working an angle. Don't be conned; you might end up dead."

"That's encouraging."
"I mean it."

Chapter Six

So Hastings and Rostov were presumably looking for Reilly—where and how they were looking, I didn't know. I wasn't cooperating with them, and I wasn't sure that they were cooperating with each other. Meanwhile, Linda and I continued to ask around, not very productively. Linda talked to her waitress friends when she wasn't teaching history, and I mostly hung around Tahawus and Newcomb and the vicinity of the mine hoping to find some trace of Reilly, but I couldn't be too obvious about it or people might think it was peculiar that an Air Force officer was spending all his time looking for Reilly and asking questions about him. They might well wonder why it was my business. I had to avoid that.

Then the banker Mac Denleigh popped up again, but at first I didn't know that he was the source of the trouble. I heard about the problem from Rabbit. He'd been contacted by the legislative liaison office of the Agency, which was handling a complaint by the congressman who represents the northern Adirondacks. The thing was vague at first—something to the effect that I was throwing my weight around—and the complaint had reached Rabbit through a roundabout chain. The congressman's local office in Plattsburgh had received the message from a clergyman and then communicated it to the Air Force, which passed it along to the commanding officer of Griffiss Air Force Base at Rome. The Griffiss staff looked into it but ran up against a wall created by the Agency. So the Air Force sent it to the CIA, and the staff of the director sent it to my boss, Rabbit. Rabbit wasn't happy. At first I thought the pushback had to do with the Linda Coyle matter, but that wasn't it.

The Agency's people on Capitol Hill found that the complainant was the Reverend Ezekiel Mordecai, pastor of the Full Gospel Tabernacle in Newcomb. I went to Newcomb and spoke to him. The church was located in a building that had started as a church, then was converted into a grocery store for a time, and was now a church again. There were brand new pews where rows of canned goods and boxes of corn flakes had once stood, and there was an altar beyond the pews. When I arrived, the pastor was standing near the front door. He had probably heard my car. I introduced myself.

The Reverend put me on the defensive immediately. "Have you come to me for spiritual advice?"

I said, "Well, no, not really."

"Maybe you need to seek the Lord and follow His commands."

"Maybe so, but I came here because I was told you had complained about me to the Congressman."

"I did, indeed, and from what I hear, you should be complained about."

"Well, Reverend, what did I do?"

"You've been harassing a member of my congregation and interfering with his employment, his job at the mine."

"Let me guess. That would be Bill Reilly, right?"

"That's correct."

I took a step or two into the church. "I'm sorry you were troubled with this, Reverend. How was the problem called to your attention? Did Mr. Reilly speak to you?"

"Yes, he did. He came to me for counseling. As I said, he's a member of my congregation."

"Well, I'd like to speak to him to see if we can work this out. Do you know where I might be able to find him? I've stopped by his house a couple of times but he wasn't home. Do you know how to reach him?"

"No, I don't."

I didn't believe him. I stayed silent and looked at him. I've found that if I can manage to be quiet long enough, people's guilt will often lead them to talk about the information I want.

Then he spoke up, "Maybe he doesn't want to talk to you."

"Maybe not."

I looked at him some more. "Is he living with you, Reverend?"

"No, he's not."

I tried another tack. "When members of your congregation come to you for counseling, do you often turn to the Congressman for help?"

"No, this is the first time I've ever done that. But you work for the federal government. You are a military officer."

"Yes, I am. Did Bill Reilly suggest to you that you contact the Congressman?"

"No. That suggestion came from my friend, Mac Denleigh, and I'm grateful to him."

I said, "Oh, I see. And how did Mr. Denleigh get involved in this?"

"I asked for his advice. He sometimes comes to a prayer group that I've organized, and after the prayer meeting I asked him. I know that he's a man who has friends in government."

"Indeed he does, Reverend, indeed he does . . . If you see Bill Reilly, would you please tell him I was looking for him?"

"I will, but I don't know whether I'll see him."

"Why not?"

"He hasn't been in church recently."

"That's too bad."

* * *

So I needed to have another conversation with Mac Denleigh.

I didn't relish it. I thought I'd scared him enough to shut him up, but apparently not. He's a reckless jerk. Did he care so much about Lord Jeffrey Amherst that he was willing to damage his son's reputation? No, I don't think so. He simply wanted to stick his finger in my eye. But first I thought I should brief Rabbit so he wouldn't be blindsided.

As little as I wanted to talk to Denleigh, I was even less eager to have this conversation with Rabbit. He didn't know about Linda's involvement with Denleigh and he wouldn't like it. I hadn't discussed it with him. He could handle the Congressman, who wouldn't really give a damn and wouldn't want to mess with the CIA, but Rabbit is usually a stickler for proper procedures. I might lose my job. Mac Denleigh truly had screwed me, probably far more than he realized.

The conversation with Rabbit was almost as bad as I had expected, but not quite. I explained that I needed the help provided by Linda and her waitress friends to identify Reilly and to try to track him down. I also told Rabbit about Denleigh's bogus objections to Linda's classroom discussion of Lord Jeffrey Amherst and that I had confronted Denleigh about it. Rabbit doesn't like phony patriots. But I didn't tell him I had used the information in Hud Denleigh's file. That went too far, and I knew it. I couldn't defend it. I thought Rabbit would have done the same thing if he had been in my shoes, but I still couldn't justify it.

Reluctantly, I made the trip to the bank. I didn't tell anyone there that I wanted to see Denleigh or where I was going. I just went up in the elevator and straight to his office. He saw me immediately.

"Captain Boudreau, what brings you here?"

"I've been to see Reverend Mordecai."

"Ah yes, he spoke to me about you." Denleigh was clearly pleased that he'd caused trouble for me.

"He told me that. He also told me that you advised him to send a complaint to the congressman."

"Well, I advised him that he could consult the congressman." Then Denleigh decided to try being tough. Sometimes you can see the transformation before your eyes. His chin jutted out. He said, "Zeke Mordecai likes to help people. Unlike you, I think, Captain."

I was willing to play by those rules. "I help people who are worthy of it, who deserve it. Zeke Mordecai helps sinners, like Bill Reilly, and sinners who have money, like you, Mr. Denleigh. It was unwise of you to get involved."

"Why was it unwise?"

"You should have realized that it creates a great risk to the reputation of your son, Hud, and your own reputation."

Denleigh pulled on the cuffs of his shirt so that his gold cufflinks became fully visible. "My lawyer tells me that your use of unproven allegations about Hud from a government file is completely improper. It is a misuse of government information, an abuse of government power."

I sat down, uninvited. "Well, speaking hypothetically, let's suppose for a moment that your lawyer is right. Let's suppose that it is improper. Maybe you could take me to court. You could sue me for slander or whatever, and we could have a trial, and at the trial the contents of Hud's file would be evidence and would be a public record. The file says, as you know, that Hud has communist affiliations. That would be published in the newspaper. Is that what you want? You mentioned unproven allegations — would you like me to prove them? Government investigators talked to people at the University of Virginia. Those same people could be summoned to testify and to describe Hud's political activity. They won't lie for you under oath. So the facts can be proven — don't fool yourself. Or perhaps you could complain to my superiors and I would lose my job. Then I'd need to defend myself and I'd have nothing further to lose by making the file public. Again, it would be in the newspapers. Do you want that? I don't see any sensible course for you except to keep your mouth shut."

Denleigh was sullen. The suit that had looked freshly creased minutes before now seemed rumpled, too big for him. He stared at his desk.

* * *

The house Hastings rented overlooked a small lake and the mountains beyond. It was far bigger than he needed, but I suppose he had a generous budget. The place was built in 1910 in the classic Adirondack style. The beams were whole logs, stripped and smoothed but not sawn into boards. He gave me a tour. The living room was two stories tall and had a very large stone fireplace with a chimney that went through the bedrooms upstairs. The heat from the chimney stones warmed those rooms and the back of the fireplace formed one wall of the dining room and heated it as well. The kitchen was basic—a gas stove and an electric refrigerator, with running water produced by a pump drawing water from the lake. The water was untreated, and if the electricity went out you lost the water along with the lights. Upstairs, in the four small bedrooms, Hastings had six beds to choose from—all of them were singles, like those in an army barracks. The place was probably intended for men to use on hunting or fishing trips, but the doctor for whom it was built had a wife. The two of them had been buried on the property, out in the side yard, but they were later dug up and moved out.

We sat down at the dining room table to talk. It was big enough to seat eight or ten, and we had room to spread out a large-scale map of the area.

He said, "We should try to find Reilly before Vasily does. Vasily will kill him."

"Now he thinks Reilly killed Kuznetsov?"

"That's what he says."

"How does he know that? Does he have any real evidence?"

"I don't think so, but you might want to be happy about it. It's better than having him think you did it."

I replied, "This doesn't make sense to me. What does Vasily know that we don't?"

Hastings stood. "I found a bottle of Kentucky bourbon in the house. Some thoughtful Christian has left it here for us. I think we should have a drink. It will make our thinking more creative."

I said, "It's only four o'clock. The sun is still up."

"It has set somewhere, and I've been reliably informed that in due course it will set here. I think we may count on it."

I asked, "Is the bourbon any good?"

"I doubt it. The people who own this house are named Murray, a Scottish name. What do Scots know about bourbon? And, besides, Scots are notoriously frugal. But let's take a chance on it."

I yielded. "Spoken like an Englishman."

Hastings went to the kitchen and got two juice glasses decorated with cartoon figures. Mine had Mickey Mouse and his had Donald Duck. He poured two fingers of bourbon into each and then sat again at the table.

We studied the map. He said, "There's no real reason why Reilly should still be in this area. He could have gone anywhere."

"Yes, but this is where his roots are. Unless he has close ties to friends somewhere else, and I haven't found any, this is where he'll feel most secure."

Hastings drank half of his bourbon. "If he's here, he must not be going out. Since he hasn't been seen, someone is taking food to him."

I agreed. "I'd bet on people at the mine. That's where he worked, those are the people he knows. But there's also a church in Newcomb where the pastor contacted a politician on Reilly's behalf."

Hastings wanted to hear about that, so I gave him a short version of the Pastor Mordecai and Mac Denleigh story. He thought we should watch both of them.

I said, "Maybe the pastor would shield Reilly, but I doubt that Denleigh would. He just wanted to cause trouble for me."

Hastings finished his bourbon. "We don't have enough manpower to watch many places, to stake out houses. Linda can't help during the week when she's teaching, and we can't cooperate with Vasily, so we won't have his help."

"Why not?"

"I don't want Vasily to find him."

"What would be so terrible if he did? I'm sure you're not competing with him."

Hastings was restless. He said, "Let's have another drink." He poured two more fingers of bourbon into our glasses. The sun was low in the west, lighting the mountain on the other side of the lake. The mountain was glowing—or maybe it was the bourbon.

Hastings and I both looked at the mountain. Then he spoke again. "If Vasily finds Reilly, he'll kill him. That's why he was sent here. Moscow told me to kill him, but I thought it was a mistake. I stalled. Another killing would cause a great deal of trouble with your government. Then the heat on me and on every other Soviet agent would be stifling. Your government knows I'm here. And Moscow doesn't really know whether Reilly killed Kuznetsov. There's no evidence. They don't know anything more than we do." He paused. "If Reilly was the source for information that Moscow needs, why would we want him dead? But that's why Vasily is here, and it means that I'm not in good standing, I'm in disfavor."

"Are you in danger?"

"I can handle it. I've performed valuable services—but I may know more than they would like me to know."

Perhaps to show that he was prepared, Hastings opened a drawer in a cabinet beside the table and took out the Webley pistol. He put it between us. It was pointed toward the lake—not at either one of us. As usual, I wasn't armed.

The bourbon had loosened him up. Me too. I asked him, "Do you like your work? Doesn't it bother you?"

The pistol was flat on the table. I stuck my index finger into the trigger guard and with the other hand pushed the barrel around in a slow circle. Hastings looked at my eyes, not the gun.

He didn't move, not a bit. I tried to remember which animal it is that immobilizes its prey by staring at it.

He was expressionless. He said, "Why should it bother me? Mostly what I do is stroll about talking with pleasant young chaps like you. Not a bad life."

I continued to toy with the gun, slowly. "What about the part with permanent consequences, the part that changes lives irrevocably, or ends them?"

Hastings smiled. "Ah, you have in mind the killings. The word, by the way, is 'kill,' a good English word. No euphemisms like 'eliminate,' or 'terminate,' or 'neutralize.' Latinisms." He raised his eyebrows in a manner that was surely intended to appear thoughtful. "That's a relatively small part of my work. It's the most dramatic part, perhaps, but nonetheless a job, a task much like any other.... Well, I confess that occasionally—very seldom, really—I confront an adversary who is so thoroughly despicable that I have no hesitation about killing him. Or her. Those cases don't bother me at all, not for a minute. But, unfortunately, I've found that many of my adversaries turn out to be dupes or dunderheads, people who got involved in situations they couldn't handle. Those people are pitiful. So I give them their due, I pity them, but I don't hesitate for them either. In this business, you can't afford to hesitate. That can be fatal. You just do your job."

"And yet, you stalled on Reilly."

"One must use professional judgment. I thought Moscow's decision was misguided."

I picked up the gun. "How many people have you killed?" It was a question I had been wanting to ask, but it may have been the bourbon talking.

"That's not the measure of my career's success."

I put down the gun and picked up the bourbon bottle. "What is the measure?"

Hastings hesitated, then said, "There's a certain satisfaction that comes from a job done well." He nodded in agreement with himself. "At one time I thought of devising a point system for evaluating my work. A large number of points would be awarded for not harming bystanders. Spare the women and children. That's practical as well as humane. Causes less trouble. Some points would be given for speed, efficiency. It's preferable that the subject go quickly. No prolonged suffering. And then another allocation of points for discretion, avoiding a scene. Public notice and unpleasantness are to be avoided. No unseemly mess. Neatness counts. But then I decided that the point system was unnecessary. An artist knows when it's done right."

He pushed his chair back from the table, stood, and left me alone in his house. I watched him go. He took the pistol with him. I washed the glasses.

* * *

The Bloomingdale bog lies between two groups of mountains. I don't call them mountain ranges because that sounds too much like the Rockies. These are Adirondack mountains. They don't impress Westerners. But they shed water that runs to the bog, and the water supports a considerable variety of plants, including tamarack, which likes to have its feet wet. Tamarack is a relative of the pines but its needles are softer and finer and it sheds them in the fall. The bog also has pitcher plants, which eat bugs that get trapped in the cup of the plant and are digested. Nature is tough. There are blueberries you can enjoy if you can get to them before the deer and the bears do, and "cotton" plants—I don't know what they are but in the fall they have fluffy white balls at the top, much more substantial than a dandelion going to seed.

The bog is large, covering several square miles. From just north of Lake Colby, near the village of Saranac Lake, it runs in a northeasterly direction toward Bloomingdale. There's a path that was once a railroad line running north and south. Sending railroads up over mountains or through tunnels is expensive, so the barons hauled fill into the bog and built a raised bed for the tracks. The bed is still there, only a few feet high. Because it's a bog, the landscape is flat, and the water spreads out and its depth doesn't fluctuate greatly. The view extends for miles until it reaches the mountains. On old maps, the railroad is called the Chateaugay line, but the tracks and the ties are long gone. The path runs straight for about five miles, a very un-Adirondack path.

Linda and I drove up to Bloomingdale and then over toward the Gabriel's potato fields to the place where the paved road crosses the path. The place isn't marked, but you can see where other cars have pulled off.

We told each other we were looking for traces of Reilly, but we knew that was far-fetched. Eventually, the Reilly excuse for the trip became a joke. We laughed about it. Linda asked me, "Do you think he might be hiding under that bridge?" I said, "Sure. Bad guys often hide under bridges." It was silly, but we didn't have leads and we were frustrated. What do you do when you've run out of ideas? You can watch TV or you can take a nice walk. The trip through the Bloomingdale bog was the better option.

The sun was setting when we got back to the car. The sky in the west was red—not just rosey, but an array of real reds. Scarlet, wine-red, magenta, carmine, maybe even puce. I've always wanted to be able to call something "puce." What other reds do you have on your palette? All of them were there. The mountains were almost black and provided contrast. The long grasses in the bog and the cotton plants had turned gold. The tamaracks, which quiver in the slightest breeze, were not moving. It would soon be cold.

It was idyllic at the bog, a romantic couple of hours. But it was time for us to go, and it was also time to get something done. But what?

* * *

It was likely, it seemed to me, that someone other than Reilly killed Kuznetsov. What would Reilly's motive have been—maybe if they had a fight or a heated enough argument, or if Kuznetsov assaulted Reilly, who then killed him in self-defense? But why would the two of them fight? Or why would Kuznetsov assault him? They were partners—Reilly was Kuznetsov's guy, and was presumably making money from the deal. Why upset the gravy wagon? I wasn't making progress.

I thought that there had probably been a falling-out within the Soviet ranks. There was clearly tension between Hastings and Rostov. Maybe there had been a change of plans or objectives within the Kremlin, or maybe my new friend, Hastings, had done the killing. He was, after all, an assassin. It was the work he was known for. Why else would he be here? Pretending to look for the killer is certainly on the list of ways for a real killer to hide. It's an old gambit, and I knew I shouldn't fall for it.

So I called the hotel in Long Lake and asked if George Spelvin had been there recently. The lady on the desk told me that he was again in residence. Rostov was still using that name.

I drove to the hotel, and the nice lady rang his room and told him he had a visitor. After a few minutes, he came lumbering down the stairs. He filled the stairway. He was even bigger up close than he had been at the Full Moon. I felt overmatched.

I said, "Would you like a cup of coffee?"

He said, "Nyet."

I asked him whether he had seen Bill Reilly.

He said, "Nyet."

His English was basic, but he knew considerably more of it than he was wasting on me. The hotel's lobby was small and there was no place for a private conversation, so I suggested that we go out on the porch to talk. He opened the door for me. I thought he was being polite, but then I realized he didn't want me behind him where he couldn't see me.

So far I had asked two questions and received two nyets. This wasn't very productive. I tried switching to French. My French was almost as limited as his English, and in response he merely shook his head. I decided to try a different approach. I thought maybe a new topic of conversation would warm him up.

I said, "Why are you using the name 'George Spelvin,' the conventional stage pseudonym?"

He said, "Why not?"

I replied, "But aren't you concerned that the name will be recognized as an alias?"

Once again, he said, "Nyet."

This approach didn't seem to be more productive.

Then he said, "You hide Reilly."

It wasn't clear to me whether that was a question or an accusation, but I think it was the latter.

I replied, "Nyet."

He smiled, very slightly.

So I said, "What are you going to do with Reilly if you find him."

He held both of his hands out in front of him, palms up, in the universal, international symbol for uncertainty. I don't think he was uncertain at all.

That was the end of our conversation. I hadn't learned a damn thing except that he was scary. He stood on the porch and watched me get into my car. When I drove away, he was still watching.

Chapter Seven

Now, for the next part of the story I'll have to rely on accounts provided by witnesses. I wasn't there. But I think I have pretty much the whole thing—part of it provided by Hastings, part by Rostov, part by the sheriff, and part by the Adirondack Medical Center.

What happened was that Rostov found Reilly before I did. As Linda and I had suspected, he'd been hiding near Tahawus. A house there was owned by one of the people who worked at the lab, a friend of Reilly's I suppose, although I hadn't found any close friends. The owner of the house had moved in with a woman, leaving his own place vacant, so he let Reilly use it. Rostov didn't know any of this, but he was watching Reverend Mordecai. He followed Mordecai to a grocery store. There were days when the Reverend bought unusually large quantities of groceries and, on those days, Rostov followed him home—except that Mordecai didn't go straight home. When he had extra supplies, he detoured for a stop at the house near Tahawus.

Rostov didn't really know who was living there—it might have been some poor pensioner, a disabled member of the Reverend's congregation who was unable to go to the store. But Rostov was suspicious, and he watched the house. The door opened in and the person who opened it for Mordecai stayed inside the house, in the shadows. On Mordecai's third visit to the house, Rostov saw enough to determine that the person inside was a young man, and with the help of binoculars he saw that the man fit the description of Bill Reilly.

The house provided a defensive position. Rostov wanted to get to Reilly before I did, but he didn't want to storm the house because a person trying to break down the front door would be an unprotected target. Reilly could stay inside, where he would not be seen, and shoot at anyone who approached. Rostov's bullet-proof vest would stop some bullets, but not all of them.

He played the percentages. A young, able-bodied man would not stay cooped up in that house indefinitely. Sooner or later Reilly would stretch his legs. And, indeed, a week after Rostov had spotted him, Reilly decided to go out. He rode a bicycle. This was a smart move because it is very difficult for an automobile to shadow a bicycle without being obvious, and it is impossible to keep up with the bicycle if you are on foot. So, the first time that Reilly went out, Rostov couldn't follow him.

But then Reilly became careless, probably overconfident. On his next outing he used a pickup truck and drove north toward Tupper Lake. Although the town is small, there is a sort of bypass around it, a road that avoids the business district and goes by the old Jewish cemetery where I had seen Reilly use the dead letter box. Reilly knew the route. But he drove past the cemetery and turned right on Route 3, toward Saranac Lake. Rostov followed. Just beyond Panther Mountain, Reilly's pickup turned right onto the Coreys Road, which leads to Axton landing. Was he returning to the scene of the crime?

Almost. But not quite. He slowed near the Axton turnoff, but then went over the bridge across Stony Creek to a parking lot. The lot provides access to the river, Raquette Falls, some campsites, and a trail that is wide and mostly flat, one of the few in the area suitable for horseback riding. It is known locally as "the Horse Trail." When Reilly stopped and parked, Rostov drove on for a couple of hundred yards, circled back, left his car on the road, and followed on foot. He didn't have his rifle with a scope, but he did have a .45 caliber pistol.

He knew that this wasn't an ideal place to do the job. There might be people around, and his car was visible on the road. But it was an opportunity. Reilly was in the open, exposed, and Rostov couldn't be sure that he'd get another chance. He thought he should take this one. It was a good place to track Reilly because the overhanging trees are trimmed to accommodate mounted riders. You can see ahead. Witnesses could be dealt with, if necessary, but they were always a nuisance. So far, he had seen no hikers. The parking lot was almost empty.

Rostov saw Reilly two hundred yards away, heading toward Raquette Falls, moving straight on the main path. He had passed a side trail that led to the lean-to and then the river. But up ahead, the trail changed. The path dipped down into a small valley and then rose again. It was harder to see far ahead.

It was to Rostov's advantage, however, that Reilly was wearing a red jacket. Foolish of him. With a rifle and scope, Rostov could easily have taken him from a hundred yards away, but the pistol was a much more limited tool. Rostov thought that, with only the pistol, it might have been better to wait in the parking lot and get a good shot when Reilly returned to the pickup truck. Waiting in the lot would have been an option. Should he return there now? Reilly's truck could provide Rostov with a shield from return fire. Or should he follow Reilly more closely, so that he didn't lose sight of the red jacket? Tailing close-up would increase the risk that Reilly would spot him, but in the parking lot there was more risk of being seen by witnesses. He decided to stay on the trail.

Then Reilly turned and was coming closer. He had reversed course, heading back. Rostov looked for a tree large enough to cover himself, but didn't see one. Dense forests seldom have big trees. There were a lot of small trees, but no big ones. The boulders farther back, glacial erratics, would have been good cover, but Rostov didn't have much time. Reilly was closing on him. Maybe he could surprise Reilly and throw him off balance.

Then Reilly made another move. He appeared to be leaving the path. If he went into the woods, Rostov would lose him. He had to act.

He called out, "Bill Reilly!" The way he said it, it sounded more like "Beel Reely!" Reilly turned, but he knew that it was a bad guy calling, and he was prepared. It's possible that he had already seen Rostov. A .38 caliber Beretta was in his hand.

Rostov got off a shot and so did Reilly. They both missed. Reilly dove behind a fallen tree. Rostov was still standing in the middle of the trail—he hadn't had time to choose the place. Reilly was lying behind the log and he was able to steady the pistol by resting it on the tree. He fired again, and missed again. He was nervous, rushing his shots. Rostov swore and got off another shot. This one hit the log near Reilly's pistol and sent splinters into his arms. He screamed in pain. Rostov, probably thinking that he had seriously wounded Reilly or perhaps killed him, took a step toward him. It was a mistake. Reilly fired again. The bullet went into Rostov's left shoulder and knocked him down.

There was a commotion on the path. Hikers coming from Raquette Falls heard the shots and the scream. It isn't entirely clear whether they were running toward the sounds or away from them, but in any event they were running. The confusion on the trail gave Reilly cover. He ran away. He wasn't wounded except for the superficial cuts on his arms. He got back to his pickup truck and drove to the office of a doctor in Long Lake.

Reilly told the nurse he had fallen into a blackberry bush. The doctor who patched him up said, "Damned funny blackberry bush, with splinters." Medical records show that the nurse took Reilly's blood pressure three times. Maybe she was trying to delay his departure from the office, or maybe she was just trying to get it right. Nobody knows where he went after that. He didn't go back to Tahawus.

In the midst of the ruckus on the trail, Rostov was up, standing on his own feet, and an Old Town Canoes T-shirt supplied by one of the hikers was now tied around his shoulder to stanch the flow of blood. Most of the hikers kept their distance because Rostov still had the pistol, but one brave or foolish soul helped him get to his car in the road beyond the parking lot. As they went through the lot, Rostov saw that Reilly's truck was already gone. Fortunately for Rostov, the house that Hastings had rented was on the Coreys road, less than five miles away, a distance that Rostov could drive using only one arm. His left arm was hanging, useless and bloody.

Hastings was at home, and he was a competent field medic. His line of work had provided experience in dressing wounds. He managed to stop the bleeding, but he wasn't going to try to remove the bullet without anesthetic and without an x-ray to tell him where it was. Rostov would have to go to a doctor and submit to questioning about a gunshot wound, but it would probably be better to avoid the closest doctor's offices. Reilly might have gone there for treatment. A confrontation in public would not be good for either of them. Thinking that Reilly would seek the familiar, a doctor closer to home, probably someone he knew near Tahawus, Hastings took Rostov in the other direction, to the Adirondack Medical Center in Saranac. He used Rostov's car. He didn't want his own car to be seen bringing in a man with a bullet wound, or to have his license number noted. He also didn't want there to be any record at a taxicab company. So, from the hospital Hastings walked to the Hotel Saranac, where he found me and told me what happened. He said that Rostov was incompetent and had botched the job.

The sheriff was called to the hospital to question Rostov, which resulted in an unsatisfactory interview. Rostov's English had suddenly become even more limited, but he did manage to say "diplomatic immunity." A deputy sheriff was told to call the Immigration and Naturalization Service, but there is no record that the call was ever made. The official police report at the office at Malone says that Rostov was struck by a bullet fired by "a person or persons unknown." So much for reconstructing history from the documentary record.

Bill Reilly was still at large. I first determined that he was no longer at the house near Tahawus. My hunch was that he was now farther away, perhaps in Syracuse or Albany, someplace bigger and with more options, but Rabbit wanted me to stay put. So I did.

It was clear to me that Rostov was a problem, a loose cannon on the deck. He was charging around attempting to commit murder. So far he had not succeeded, but he was trying to kill my witness, Bill Reilly. I wanted Reilly to talk; I wanted answers for some of the open questions, especially about what the Soviets were after at the mine. It occurred to me that Rostov might be less concerned about the death of Kuznetsov than about silencing Reilly. I couldn't let that happen.

For the time being, Rostov was staying with Hastings, recuperating from the gunshot wound. Hastings didn't like Rostov and didn't respect him, but they worked for the same employer.

* * *

Two weeks later, Linda and I had dinner at the Full Moon. We were no longer concerned about being seen together. People could get used to it. And the place wasn't crowded at dinnertime—we were able to talk. There was a seafood quesadilla filled with shrimp and other good things. Remarkably good for a place so far from the sea.

Halfway through dinner Linda said, "I've been thinking, Joe. Why are you here?"

I was thick. "To have dinner with you."

She smiled. "No, I mean why were you sent to the Adirondacks?"

She already knew the answer, but I reviewed it. "Because the Soviets had design info on the airplane, the TFX, and because our intel people picked up that Kuznetsov was here. So my boss figured the data might be leaking from the lab at Tahawus. Now that Hastings and Rostov are here, that theory looks good. The Soviets are putting significant resources into the operation."

Linda closed her eyes. "What if it's a diversion, a distraction designed to cover up the real source of the leaks?"

"It could be. That's a tactic in military strategy called a 'feint.'"

We had considered that, of course. The data could have come from the airplane manufacturers working on the design, or even from the Pentagon. But there wasn't any evidence of that. Both the Air Force and the FBI were investigating, but they hadn't found anything. And I had seen Reilly pass documents to Kuznetsov through the dead letter box. This was where the action was. I told Linda all of this.

She said, "It's just a thought." She paused. "But why are the Soviets so obvious here? Both Hastings and Rostov? They're not being very subtle. Hastings even approached you, came over and talked to you. Why?"

I said, "Maybe he thought it was better that we didn't shoot each other. Once Kuznetsov was killed, they had an understandable concern here. They had already lost one agent. Maybe they wanted to know how or why that happened. Maybe they even wanted retribution."

"Then you're in danger?"

"Sure. We know that. But I think my contact with Hastings reduces that risk. It helps to prevent a miscalculation, a misunderstanding."

She persisted. "But what if he's playing you. What if he wants you to be distracted from the real source of the leak?"

"Well, then he's doing a damn good job of it. I'm distracted alright."

Chapter Eight

Then I got a surprise. Rabbit Maranville came to visit. I suppose I should have been pleased to see him, but I thought his presence here was insulting—I thought he was checking up on me. And he was. But then I decided that maybe I shouldn't be so defensive—maybe he came because the case was important and he was demonstrating that by giving it his personal attention. Or maybe he just wanted a vacation (I don't think so).

Rabbit was staying in a big grey-green clapboard house on Raquette Lake, south of Long Lake and west of Blue Mountain Lake. The place was at least an hour and a half away from Saranac by car, so he wasn't exactly underfoot. Rabbit was the guest of an old friend, General Ironwood, fondly known as Iron Pants Ironwood. I think the General has CIA in his background somewhere.

The house is certainly inaccessible. I had to take a boat to get there—no road goes to the far side of the lake. The Raquette Lake village has a general store, a couple of houses, and not much else. Sagamore, the great camp of the Vanderbilts, is nearby, a couple of miles outside the town, but it isn't on the big lake. The Vanderbilts had their own lake.

A launch piloted by Iron Pants himself met me at the store's dock. That was a good thing because I would not have been able to find the house. The grey-green paint on the clapboard had weathered so that some patches were dark green, some exposed to more sun had faded to a lighter green, and some were a neutral grey. It was beautiful from up close, but out on the lake the effect was to make the house almost invisible. Nestled in behind the pines, the variegated color worked like camouflage. I didn't ask the General whether that was intentional. I suppose the paint may be an artistic achievement created by a decorator at a cost of $50,000. What do I know?

The day was windy and there was a chop on the lake. In another week or two the lake would start to freeze. The launch smacked oncoming waves with a solid thunk. It was a good thing that I grew up here and knew what to expect, and that the General knew how to handle a boat. We headed toward the eastern shore, near the inlet of the Marion River.

In the nineteenth century, rich people from New York City took trains that brought them to Raquette Station, near where the store is now. From the station's dock on the shore of the lake, a steam-powered boat picked them up, took them across the lake, and up the Marion River to a landing where their servants transferred the luggage to another railroad—a short, very short line, only a mile or two long—that carried them to a dock on Utowanna Lake where they were met by another steamboat and transferred their luggage again. The second boat steamed through the length of Utowanna and Eagle Lakes and connecting streams, eventually reaching Blue Mountain Lake, where there were hotels. The buildings are all gone now. Back to nature.

The mouth of the Marion River has created a long point, extending far into Raquette Lake, and our boat headed toward the point. It looked like we were going to the river, but we stopped about halfway along the inlet. The General and I walked from his private dock, up cut-stone steps to the house. Rabbit was sitting in a wicker chair on the front porch. The decor was informal. A fly swatter hung from a nail in the wall directly above Rabbit's head.

He was smoking a pipe. As was often the case when I met with Rabbit, he pointed the stem of the pipe away from him and waved it around aimlessly, or what appeared to me to be aimlessly. This time he seemed to aim the pipe at a large pine tree near the lake. He moved it in small circles and then up and down, and then he started over. I thought this was peculiar, but probably just a nervous tic. Eventually, however, I saw that he was writing "Maranville" in the air. He didn't write Rabbit.

He greeted me. "How's the fishing?"

I said, "Do you mean literal fish, like pike and such, or were you asking about my work?"

At that point the General said, "I'm going inside to help Ellen, and I'll leave it to you comrades-at-arms to deal with these important matters."

When the General had gone inside, Rabbit replied, "I'm prepared to accept whatever you want to tell me. I'm comfortably seated here with a good view of the lake, and this coat is warm, so I'm easy. I'm interested in pike, but I'm also willing to listen to what you might have about Soviet spies."

With Rabbit, you have to be careful. When you think he's just being playful, or isn't paying attention, he will pounce. He's so practiced in evasion that he does it habitually. He answers everything as if he is testifying before a congressional committee.

I gave it a try. "Can't tell you much about pike; I've been too busy searching the woods looking for Bill Reilly and Vasily Rostov."

"Ah, yes. And how about Ev Hastings?"

"I know where he is. Or at least I think I do."

"May I meet him?"

I was surprised. "Hastings? I assume I could arrange that."

"Please."

"Is it appropriate for me to ask why?"

"No, I don't suppose it is appropriate, but I'll answer nonetheless, for instructional purposes." He took a small pen knife out of his pocket and dug at the ashes in his pipe. "I want to take the measure of the man. He has a considerable reputation. I want to see what he's made of."

"Okay. I'll set it up. Or I'll try to. I can tell you that he comes across as an English gentleman, or tries to, dresses like one, talks like one, mostly. Of course, it might be an act."

Rabbit used his small smile. "I can tell you he didn't go to either Oxford or Cambridge."

"Is that important?"

"To an Englishman, it is." He stood. "I'd like to see the titanium mine, but first Mrs. Ironwood has prepared a fine lunch here in this beautiful setting."

I said, "Oh." And I'm afraid that was all I said.

Rabbit looked at the floor. His chin was near his shirt, which was a wool plaid, probably Adirondack gear provided by the Agency's wardrobe department. Then he said, "Of course we can't discuss business during lunch." He paused. "Too bad Linda isn't here to enjoy the lunch."

I was surprised again. The joining of the two remarks, about talking business and about Linda, told me he was concerned about her role. I said, "What would you like to know about Linda?"

He replied, "I work for the CIA. We know many things. Unfortunately, not everything."

I had heard it before. They didn't know as much as they wanted to know but they often extracted information by pretending to know things. I could have asked what he objected to about Linda's involvement in my work, but I knew that would be dangerous, confrontational. Or I could have told him that Linda thought Hastings was charming, thus telling him that she had been in contact with Hastings, but that would have been even more provocative. So I decided to let it rest with his assertion that the Agency knew "many things," letting him have the last word.

But Rabbit wasn't finished with it. He said, "After lunch we need to have a conversation about what Linda has to do with all this."

He seemed to want to spoil my digestion. So I decided to spoil his. "I need help, Rabbit, and the Agency isn't providing it. One person can't cover the whole Adirondacks."

He said, "We don't recruit civilians to do the job, especially with no screening or training. For Christ's sake, Joe! What is this? Amateur hour?"

"I was hoping you could meet Linda, sir, talk with her, see how helpful she can be."

"It's not my job to evaluate your lovers. I'm not your father, I'm a public official. And I'm an official who has a duty to protect national security. What in the hell ever happened to secrecy?"

"It is not a secret, sir, that there are Russian agents operating in this neighborhood. The Russians themselves have seen to that. Kuznetsov's death was reported in the local newspapers, although he hadn't been identified yet. Rostov was in a shootout, was treated in a local hospital, and has claimed diplomatic immunity. Hastings parades around in local restaurants and introduces himself to librarians. They haven't been exactly inconspicuous. Hastings visited me at the hotel more than once—most recently after he delivered a gunshot victim to the hospital. So what is it I'm supposed to keep secret?"

Rabbit fiddled with his pipe. "Yes. It seems the cat is out of the bag." He put down the pipe and said, "After lunch." He started to go inside, but then he stopped. "It's interesting, isn't it, that the Russians are being so conspicuous. I wonder why."

Linda was not mentioned again—until much later.

* * *

So Rabbit wanted to meet Hastings. The easiest way to arrange that was also the most straightforward. I went to see Hastings and asked him whether he would be willing to do it. To my surprise, he was reluctant. He hadn't seemed hesitant about meeting with me when he initiated contact by coming over to my table at the Full Moon, and then he had dinner with me and with Linda. I was seeing Hastings more often than I saw my cousins. So why didn't he want to meet Rabbit? In retrospect, I truly think he was a bit afraid of Rabbit. Not afraid for his physical safety, but afraid that he'd be outwitted. I wasn't a threat to Hastings—I was a neophyte agent, and he knew that—but Rabbit had long experience and was known to be shrewd. He had a reputation as a spymaster. Hastings may also have been reluctant because he knew things that he didn't want to discuss. It's always safer to avoid such subjects than to lie.

After some thought, however, Hastings relented and agreed to do it. He invited us to come to the house at Coreys, but Rabbit preferred a more neutral, more public site. The Adirondack Museum at Blue Mountain Lake is approximately half-way between Coreys and the General's camp on Raquette Lake, and the museum has a building exhibiting Adirondack transportation in the 19th century. The display includes a private railroad car that a Golden Age grandee used for trips to and from the mountains. It suited my sense of humor to have Rabbit and Hastings meet in the private railroad car. A twenty-dollar bill to one of the museum guards arranged for the car to be closed to the public for thirty minutes. No harm done. So they met.

Rabbit had not wanted me to be present for the meeting, but Hastings had insisted on it. I was there.

Rabbit spoke first. "Ah, the legendary Evelyn Hastings."

"You flatter me. Perhaps 'the notorious Ev Hastings' would be closer to the mark." Hastings settled himself into one of the heavy upholstered chairs bolted to the floor. "And now I'm privileged to meet the very anonymous Charles Maranville, known as Rabbit. Not 'the Rabbit,' just 'Rabbit.' You think we don't know about you, but we do. Yours is a much more exclusive sort of fame."

Rabbit put his hands into the side pockets of his tweed jacket and looked at the carved mahogany paneling. He said, "There's a novel notion, 'exclusive fame.' That's appealing. There should be more of it."

Hastings pursued it. "Oh, it won't do to be known by the man on the street, the hoi polloi. You, sir, have the advantage of being known only in select circles."

But Rabbit was not disposed to play games. He came to the point. "Mr. Hastings, I'm troubled. Of course, I'm often troubled by your activities, or by the reports I receive about them, but I usually think I understand the reasons for what you do. I may not approve of those reasons, but I think I know your motives and they make sense to me. In this instance, however, I'm damned if I can figure out why you're here. What do you expect to get out of it, expect to gain?"

"It's quite simple, really. We tend our wounded, and we do not leave the bodies of our soldiers on the battlefield."

Rabbit wasn't having it. "Nonsense! Or perhaps it would be more palatable if I said poppycock or balderdash. You leave them on the battlefield all the time. It just depends on what's convenient."

Hastings laughed. "I'm very glad you didn't say bullshit."

Rabbit replied, "I'm perfectly capable of saying that."

"I'm sure. But my colleague, Pavel Kuznetsov, was murdered here on your soil, and you might concede that we would be at least moderately interested in who did that and why."

"And were you not capable of handling that? Why did your superiors think it necessary to send Vasily Rostov as well?"

"I suppose it was too much for me. You see before you a humiliated old man."

Now it was Rabbit's turn to laugh. "I don't believe that for a minute. Kuznetsov was not a high level agent. We know that. He was a journeyman. It was an annoyance to lose him, no doubt, but not a major blow. And I'm sure you would like to know why he was killed, but I suspect you already have a pretty good idea about that. I think it's likely that there are those in the Soviet Union who wanted him dead."

Hastings replied, "Are you suggesting that I killed him?"

"The possibility had occurred to me."

"Balderdash!, to use your quaint language. If I'd killed him, you'd say 'good riddance' and you wouldn't be here now and neither would I. I'd be long gone. So let's be serious and talk about the real world."

Rabbit paused, only briefly, and then said, "Alright, fine. In the real world, what do you hope to learn about the mine at Tahawus?"

"Ah. You know as well as I that there are some things we can't discuss."

"We know Moscow has design details of the TFX, details we don't want you to have, so what is there that we can't discuss?"

"I'm not going to confirm any of that, or comment on what we have and what we don't have."

"No, of course not. You're far too experienced to do that."

Hastings continued, "But I had hoped that we might be able to cooperate in trying to locate Bill Reilly. I think we both have an interest in talking to him, but Joe has not been cooperative."

"Good. I'm glad to hear that; that means he was following instructions."

"Very sensible of him, no doubt. Not very productive, but very sensible."

Rabbit tried again, "Why is Rostov here? He seems to be more interested in shooting at Reilly than in talking with him. Have you assigned the wet work to him?"

"Wet work! How colorful! You've been reading too many novels."

"I read no novels at all, Mr. Hastings. I have better things to do. Mostly, pursuing Soviet agents."

"Quite. Well, I wish you Godspeed with that."

"Fine." Rabbit was all business. "Now that Reilly is no longer bringing you documents from the lab at the mine, perhaps you and Rostov are hoping to cultivate a new source, to establish a new channel of communication. That would seem to be a logical inference."

"Perhaps."

Rabbit continued, "And, if we find that your side has new information, information that has come into its possession since the death of Kuznetsov and Reilly's departure from the mine, then we would conclude that the material came from elsewhere."

"Yes, that would seem to follow, if you did in fact find that Moscow was in possession of new material. But, I suppose, the new source need not be elsewhere."

"So there might be another traitor here?"

"No doubt it is always wise to be on the lookout for traitors, wherever they might be." He shook his head, "It's so hard to exclude possibilities."

Rabbit stood, and I followed. Rabbit said, "Well, this has been a pleasant conversation. Please give my regards to your colleagues."

Hastings replied, "I have certainly enjoyed it. It was a pleasure to meet you, Director."

After we left the museum, Rabbit said to me, "Hastings was polite. Not very informative, but polite."

I asked him, "What did we learn?"

Rabbit paused. "I thought the most interesting thing was his sparring about whether the source of the leak might be elsewhere. He seemed eager to suggest that material might still be coming from the mine. Whether he really hoped to misdirect us or whether he merely wanted to give that impression is an open question. It's certainly a possibility that there's a source elsewhere."

"It's guesswork, Rabbit."

"Yes, of course it is."

The next morning I drove Rabbit to Tahawus to look at the mine. We didn't see anything interesting. He didn't visit the lab because he didn't want to start talk about the CIA investigating it. That afternoon he returned to Washington.

Chapter Nine

Later I went to Coreys to meet with Hastings. He said, "Maranville is a buttoned-up old buzzard."

I said, "Yeah. He is. He told me he liked you."

"What did he get from it?"

"Nothing." And then I changed the subject. "I need to talk to Rostov. He's not at the Long Lake Hotel, under the Spelvin name or any other so far as I can tell. Where is he?"

"He's holed-up in a motel in Tupper Lake, nursing his wound. Are you sure that all you want to do is talk to him?"

I think that Hastings's concern was sincere. I wanted to see if he would tell me more. "Yeah. I think so. But I might need to ask him to leave the country."

"He wouldn't take that well."

"How much English does he understand?"

Hastings said, "All of it. He can also speak it when he wants to. Why do you want to talk to him?"

"I want to know whether he's trying to capture Reilly or to kill him. I think he wants to shut him up."

"Why would he want to do that?"

I gave him the obvious answer, the truthful one. "Because Reilly knows something your side would rather not reveal."

"If that were the case, why wouldn't I be trying to silence him?"

"Maybe you're working on it, but you're just more subtle and skillful."

Hastings stood and paced the room. He said, "You're very kind, but you give me too much credit. If you're planning to meet with Vasily, be very careful. Don't push him. For God's sake, don't get into a shootout with him. He's a professional. Reilly was lucky and was able to shoot from cover. The odds are you won't be that lucky."

"Where should I try to meet him? I don't think I want to go to his motel room."

"No, you don't. He's a big man and even with his wound he could kill you with his bare hands."

"Thanks." I knew what Hastings said was true.

Then he had a suggestion. "What about meeting with him here?"

"That's an idea." I liked the idea, but I suggested an improvement on it. "I think he might be more willing to talk if you weren't around. I think you outrank him."

"Yes, I do." Hastings paced again. "What if he thought that he was coming here to meet with me, but it turned out that only you were here instead? It would add an element of surprise, which would be to your advantage. This is familiar territory for you. You'd be more comfortable here than he would."

"I like that idea."

So that's what we arranged. Hastings called Rostov, who agreed to come to the house at Coreys the next day at three. Hastings told me to arrive at two-thirty and that he would already be gone. The front door would be unlocked and I should let myself in.

* * *

I didn't sleep well, and there was a cold rain when I left the hotel, so instead of walking down the street to the Full Moon for lunch I got my car from the hotel's parking lot and drove to the Wawbeek Lodge, a resort located on Upper Saranac Lake near Panther Mountain. The Wawbeek usually served residential guests only, but I went to high school with the owner, so I had special privileges, and it was closer to Coreys. I wanted to be sure to get to the house by two-thirty. I was eager.

As I ate lunch, I thought about what I would ask Rostov. There were two main things I wanted to know: whether he killed Kuznetsov, and whether he knew where Reilly was. He probably wouldn't tell me either one, voluntarily. And I couldn't compel him to talk. Could I trick him? I didn't see how. I wasn't trained in interrogation, and I didn't know how to do it. Maybe, if I confronted him, he'd blurt something out. That didn't seem likely. Or maybe he'd shoot me. That seemed more likely.

By the time I finished lunch, the rain had stopped. The schedule gave me half an hour to move the furniture in the house to suit my purposes. Hastings had suggested that I create a defensive position. His concern for my safety did nothing to reassure me. The stone fireplace is huge, faces the living room, and is in a direct line of sight from the front door. You can walk around either side of the fireplace to get from the living room to the dining room. The stone would stop bullets, and I could have hidden behind it, but someone needed to answer the knock on the door. Rostov, who was expecting Hastings, would be surprised when he saw me, and he'd be careful about entering. Besides, I didn't want to shoot him. That's not my job. I wanted to get information. He was worth more to me alive than dead.

So I decided that we we'd sit in the living room. But I certainly wanted to have a gun nearby. Would it be better to put it on a table, in plain sight, or should I put it in a drawer or under a pillow? Having it in plain sight might reassure him, but it would guarantee that I wouldn't be able to get to it in time if I needed it. He would move more confidently than I. It occurred to me that, if I had two guns, I could put one in plain sight and the other under a pillow. But I didn't have two guns. I'm an amateur. So I put it under a pillow on the sofa.

Rostov arrived on time. The first thing he said was, "Where's Hastings?"

He stayed at the door, not entering. I said, "He wasn't here when I got here. Anyway, I wanted to be able to talk with you, just the two of us."

He didn't move. "I don't think so." His English was now fluent—heavily accented, but fluent.

I played the host. "Come in. Why don't you sit in the comfortable chair and I'll take the sofa?" I stepped back, making room for him to enter.

He came in, but replied, "I will stand."

I said, "Okay, if you want to."

I sat. He was looming over me. I asked, "What happened between you and Bill Reilly?"

"He shot me. Do you see my arm in a sling?"

"Witnesses say you also shot at him."

"I was defending myself."

"Maybe. But we don't like shooting here. We have laws. You're a guest in this country, and you could be sent home. Innocent people could have been hurt."

"This country has shooting on the streets every day. Look at the television." He paused. "Someone shot Kuznetsov."

I changed the subject. "What does Reilly know?"

"What?"

"I think Reilly knows something that you don't want him to talk about, so you want to either kill him or scare him so much that he'll keep his mouth shut."

At that point, he must have decided that the best defense was to go on offense. He said, "Why did you kill Kuznetsov?"

"I didn't."

"You were there."

"At Axton landing? Yes, I was. I found the body."

"Dead, or alive?"

"Dead."

"Why should I believe that? He was my friend."

I said, "I'm sorry for your loss." It probably didn't sound sincere. That was not a good move. His face changed. Not for the better. Before, it was menacing. Now it became something worse. He was still standing, still looming over me. I tried to get up from the sofa. I stumbled and made a move toward the pillow that covered my gun. He saw the move. With his right hand, he pulled a pistol out of the sling on his left arm. His gun fired. Or I thought it did. I heard a gunshot. Then he dropped to the floor.

An open staircase runs along one wall of the living room. It goes to a balcony at the second floor level, and the balcony provides access to the bedrooms. I looked up. Hastings was on the balcony with a short rifle in his hands.

He had shot Rostov in the back of his head, in the area of the occipital bone. The big man was felled like a steer in a slaughterhouse. I was speechless.

Hastings came down the stairway, slowly. He didn't say anything. Then he walked over to me, reached out a hand, and helped me up off the sofa.

He said, "You okay?"

I replied, "You killed him!"

"Of course I did. Damned good thing, too. If he'd killed you, there would've been an international crisis — headlines, 'Russian agent kills CIA man, on American soil.' Imagine it. And your government would have come down on me. I'm renting this house, and I'm much more famous than Vasily Rostov. And the Soviets would have disowned me — they would have said, 'He's British. He doesn't work for us.'"

"Jesus, Ev! This isn't what I wanted."

"Did you want to stay alive? He was going to kill you. You had no chance going for that gun."

"I didn't know you were here."

"It was better that way. You acted normally. You didn't look up."

Rostov was bleeding only a bit. I said, "There isn't much blood."

"No, there wouldn't be. The bullet went straight down into the body. There's no exit wound. He was looking down at you." He pointed at me. "You have to know these things."

"What do we do with him now?"

"The best thing for all of us, the best thing for international relations, will be to have him disappear. I'll tell Moscow that I don't know where he went."

"How do we make him disappear?"

"All we need is a deep body of water and some concrete blocks. The Adirondacks has plenty of both."

I didn't know much about disposing of bodies, but I knew the territory. "The Stony Creek Ponds are pretty shallow."

"I'll need your help. He is too heavy for me to handle him alone. I'm an old man."

"Old, but still lethal....I'm grateful. You're right, he was going to kill me."

"Yep. That was how I saw it."

I looked at Rostov again. "There's some blood."

"We'll need to clean that up. Mr. Murray isn't going to want to have a stain. And it would be careless of us to leave evidence lying around. Unprofessional." He looked at a map. "Is there a reservoir somewhere nearby? I don't want to have to drive the body all over the Adirondack Park."

"There's a Coreys cemetery just a couple of hundred feet from here. Maybe there's some space available."

"Digging a grave would be pretty conspicuous. And whatever family we chose might be curious about the new relative they acquired. I think I prefer the reservoir."

"There's a dam up at Franklin Falls, north and east of Bloomingdale. They dammed up the Saranac River. I don't know how deep it is. There's not much need for reservoirs in the Adirondacks, what with all the lakes."

"Yes, point taken."

* * *

I picked up my hat and coat. "Hastings, this is serious. This is covering up a murder and I'm helping you do it."

"You are misinformed, young Joseph. The death of Vasily was not a murder. Haven't you ever heard of self-defense?"

"Sure, but he wasn't about to kill you."

"Under the great body of law that you have inherited from the mother country, one is permitted to use deadly force to save the life not only of yourself but of any innocent person, and you are, my boy, an innocent if ever there was one."

I shifted my ground. "But don't we have a duty to report the death?"

"Perhaps." The bourbon bottle had been left sitting out. Hastings put it away, and said, "But if we did that, the KGB would come after me. They wouldn't stop."

"I'm a government official. I have a duty."

"If I thought you'd report this, I'd have to prevent that. And then my saving of your life would have been to no avail. I would regret that, but I would do it."

"Oh.... But we're going to be covering this up, concealing it."

"Yes, and I hope we do a good job of it. Confession may be good for the soul, but it certainly isn't good for the life." Hastings adopted a thoughtful pose. "Our method of burial may be somewhat unusual, but perhaps we could claim that it's a religious practice, protected by your admirable freedom of religion, as is the use of peyote in religious services. Which I have always envied. We could claim that our sect practices ritual burial at sea and that a large lake was as close as we could come to a sea. When Percy Shelley drowned while sailing off the coast of Italy and there was a dispute with the authorities concerning the disposition of his body, his friends burned it on a pyre on the beach."

"You are very erudite."

"In my line of work, old boy, one takes an interest in these things."

So Hastings and I had to dispose of the body. It turned out to be a complicated process. When the disposal in question is six feet three or four inches tall (or long) and weighs about two hundred and thirty pounds, you don't just throw the thing over your shoulder, go out into the middle of a lake, and drop it in. Apart from the obvious problem of handling a package of that size, some extra care was required because of the special sensitivities, the need for discretion.

Hastings instructed me. "The first thing we do is strip him, then burn the clothes and bury those ashes. In identifying a body, clothes often provide useful clues. Some of Vasily's things are Russian-made."

I replied. "Even if there was only a skeleton, the KGB would know immediately who it is. They won't be missing many men of his size, or many in the Adirondacks."

"True. We can be sure one thing, the Russians will be looking for him. They don't like to lose men without knowing where they've gone. If someone were holding him, they'd be very concerned. More concerned than if he were dead." Hastings mused. "We might do better to cut off his hand and mail it to them."

"Are you serious?"

"Probably not, but it's a thought." Hastings looked around the room, as if searching for something. "We also need to make a few trips to what you call hardware stores. We need concrete blocks and heavy chain, and a strong padlock. And we don't want to buy all of those things at the same store—that might attract attention. It might look suspicious, but you can use the same supplies to anchor a boat."

"We could get the concrete blocks from Tupper Lake Supply, and then the chain and lock from Fortune Hardware, only about three blocks from there."

Hastings said, "That's too close. I don't want stores in the same town."

"You're very careful."

"Any job worth doing is worth doing well. As I've said, neatness counts." He chuckled, which I thought was overdoing it.

I said, "I think you've done this before."

"There's an instruction manual." As we left, he locked the front door of the house. "Don't want intruders. And we have to get rid of Vasily's car — soon. Did I say that we need a boat? Preferably a flat bottom rowing boat about sixteen feet long."

"We could rent one."

"No. Rental agencies keep records. It's better to buy a used one from a private seller. We should look in the classified advertisements in the local papers. I want a metal boat. Wood absorbs things. If we have to use wood, we'll burn that too."

"The man will get ripe while we are doing all this."

"Well, then we should move quickly."

We took Rostov's car to the parking lot at the motel where he had been staying. We wore gloves. The car would be just one more thing he had left there, and it would be returned to the rental company. Then we went to Tupper Lake Supply and bought fifteen concrete blocks. Hastings said it was better to buy more than we needed rather than just enough to weight down a body. We could leave the extras on a vacant lot in town where someone would help themselves to them soon enough. Then Hastings bought twelve feet of heavy steel chain and a ten dollar lock from Aubuchon Hardware in Saranac Lake. He handled the transaction because they knew me there. He said the clerk commented, "I'll bet you're going to lock something up." Hastings replied, "They're not going to get into the boathouse this year." The clerk pursued it, probably just being friendly. "Got some good boats in there, do you?" Hastings gave the man the hard look and said, "None that I want to lose." That ended the conversation.

Then he decided that we needed a pickup truck, one big enough to hold a boat in the bed with a large bundle underneath the boat. He said we didn't have to buy the truck. He permitted me to rent it.

Getting the boat required a half-day trip. Hastings found

what we were looking for in the Plattsburgh newspaper. A farmer near there had an old metal rowboat for sale, cheap. I bought it and paid cash—Hastings thought it would be better if the farmer didn't remember that it was bought by an Englishman.

Once we had the truck, and the boat, and the chain and lock, and the concrete blocks, and the naked corpse, having already disposed of his clothes, we were ready to drive the whole shebang up to Franklin Falls. The lake was not yet frozen over, but it soon would be. We gave considerable thought to the time of day when this could be done with the least likelihood of being seen. We finally settled on about five a.m. on a Tuesday morning, as if we wanted to be out on the lake fishing by sunrise. We hoped to be done by seven.

The concrete blocks weren't chained to the body until after we got to the boat launch because otherwise the package would have been too heavy and awkward to handle. So we decided to put it all together at the Falls, and then wrestle the whole production into the rowboat. It would have been an interesting spectacle if anyone had been watching.

We tried attaching the blocks to him on the shore, but found that we couldn't do it until we got out on the lake. Too awkward. And the bottom of the rowboat needed to be flat so we could stand up when we were lifting it all out of the boat. Would the concrete blocks go into the water first, or the corpse first? We did the blocks first because he was heavier than they were and we wanted the blocks out of the way when we were struggling with the body.

During the discussion of these arrangements, I figured out that Hastings had, in fact, never done this before. He was making it up as he went along. We would have been better off dumping Rostov in the woods and letting the bears have him. By the time we got to Franklin Falls, I wished we had done that.

I said, "Hastings, you're a fraud."

He replied, "Are you only now discovering that, dear boy?"

"How do you get away with it?"

"Panache, dear boy, panache."

I said, "Well, get your panache into that goddamn boat and let's dump this sucker."

He stayed in character. "Rightee-oh."

Attaching the concrete blocks would have been easier when the body was stable. When we took the clothes off, Rostov was stiff as a board. Rigor mortis had set in. His arms and legs were rigid and we had to cut and tear some of the clothes to get them off. Having him stiff was helpful when we carried him out to the shed behind the Murray house for temporary storage, but by the time we got the truck and loaded him in for the trip to Franklin Falls, he was flexible again. Limp, even. This made him harder to handle. Working with a board or an assemblage of boards is relatively straightforward, but attaching chains to spaghetti requires creativity. It was a damn good thing that we didn't have spectators.

Eventually, we completed our work at the Falls, got back to Coreys, and finished off the Murray bourbon bottle. We then still had to dispose of the rowboat and return the rented truck. We took the boat to Pickerel Pond, swamped it, and left it in the pond half-filled with water. The pond is secluded, and intrepid fishermen sometimes leave boats there. They would be happy to use ours. The truck was simply a matter of returning a rented truck. No fuss, no bother.

So it amounted to this: Hastings had killed Rostov, quickly, without hesitation and without second thoughts. That focused my mind. The man really was an assassin. Maybe he would do the same thing to me.

Chapter Ten

Having been out very early in the morning, I went back to Hot Sara, cleaned up, and took a nap. That night, Linda and I went out to dinner. Halfway through our meal, she said, "You seem distracted. Is something wrong?"

I said, "Oh, maybe I'm just tired. My work hasn't been going well."

"Anything major?"

"Nah, just a few bumps in the road."

"Dangerous bumps?"

"What makes you think that?"

"The dark circles under your eyes."

"I need more sleep."

I didn't want to scare Linda. I was also worried that if I gave her the full story she'd be horrified, walk away, and not have anything more to do with me. That would have been a sensible way for her to respond. Maybe I owed her honesty. I probably did. But I couldn't face the prospect of losing her. I made excuses for myself—I told myself that I'd suffered enough, that I'd been through too much. CIA employees have secrets they can't disclose to their lovers or spouses. So I just kept quiet and tried to reassure her. I couldn't face it.

But she knew something was wrong. To be helpful, she suggested that I organize a posse of Boudreaus to help me look for Bill Reilly. It made sense to turn to family, but that carried some risk. Rabbit was already uneasy about the help I was getting from Linda. I had to be careful about how I went about it, but I needed new sources of information.

I worked my way through a few Boudreaus before I got to Uncle Clarence. Clarence was working in Malone at the International Border Company, just south of the St. Lawrence River, about an hour's drive north of Saranac Lake. I suppose I could have used the telephone, but that would have been impersonal. I'd been away from here for quite a while, and it had probably been at least ten years since I had last seen Clarence. I needed to re-establish trust. The mission was sensitive and I had to be careful. So I made the trip.

It was a long conversation. After we had talked about the weather and the state of muskie fishing on the St. Lawrence, I got down to business.

"So, Clarence, do you happen to know a young fella named Bill Reilly?"

"Well, I should know him. He's sort of shirttail kin, I guess. Ethel is a cousin—a first cousin, I think—of Helen LaPierre Reilly." Ethel is Clarence's wife. "They're both LaPierres. And Bill, I believe, is one of Helen's kids. But I don't really know the boy."

"Hah, that's interesting. I'm trying to locate Bill. Would Ethel know where I could find him?" I had prepared a story about repaying money borrowed from Reilly, but I didn't have to use it, which was a good thing. If I dangled money but then got Reilly arrested, I would probably not be welcome at the next Boudreau reunion. But I knew that, by the time this was over, I might have to burn some bridges. There was already the Rostov matter, for example.

Clarence, however, was not inquisitive. He replied, "I'll ask her," and then he called out to Ethel. When she came into the living room, he said, "My love, is Bill Reilly one of your cousin Helen's boys?"

She said, "He is. What's he done now?"

I'm glad to say that Clarence answered that question, or failed to answer it. "Joe, here, is trying to find Bill. Do you know where he is these days?"

She looked at me. I had to say something. "He worked at the titanium mine in Tahawus, as a draftsman, but he's left there now and I don't know where he is."

Ethel is a pleasant lady, gracious. "As it happens, I visited with Helen last week. She's at Alex Bay now, just up the river past Morristown. We were bringing each other up to date on our children, and I think she told me that Bill recently moved to Canada. Yes, I'm sure she did. But he's somewhere near, in one of the smaller towns just on the other side of the river. A French name. Not far from Wellesley Island."

Clarence suggested, "Maybe Gananoque?"

"Yes, that's right."

As casually as I could muster, I said, "Do you know where he's working there?"

Ethel was vague. First she said, "No, I don't think so." Then she hesitated, thought a bit, and said, "Wait now, I'm pretty sure Helen said something about him working at a marina or a boat rental place."

That would fit. I had asked Langley to check with both U. S. and Canadian customs officials, and there was no record of a William or Bill Reilly having entered Canada. Of course, he might have used a phony passport with a different name, but that would have required some preparation and expense. It was a lot easier and safer to just float across the river. All you really need is a small boat, even a canoe, and then you might well end-up in a marina or a boatyard. There's a whole culture of river rats—fishermen, "guides," smugglers—who work the river, and there's frequent turnover in that population. Not many questions are asked.

I took the bridge across the St. Lawrence just north of Watertown. The view from the bridge is beautiful. You have a rare opportunity to see life on the occupied islands in the middle of the river. Those small islands look idyllic, but I think it must, in fact, be a pain in the ass to live on an island. It sounds romantic until you think about it. How many prospective sales of those islands fall through when the purchaser sobers up? I suppose the island would work for a couple of days, to take a break from your seven-room condo in a Toronto or NYC high-rise.

Gananoque, right on the river, is pretty much one main street, a public park, and a harbor with the usual trades that cater to boat owners. It didn't take long to find him. When Reilly saw me walk into the boatyard, he didn't turn and run, but he looked like he was considering it.

I said, "Hello, Mr. Reilly, are you living in Canada now?"

He mumbled, "I'm busy working."

"Well, you should take a little time to let the Canadians know you're here. I've contacted Canadian Immigration, and they tell me there's no record of a William Reilly entering the country. They like to keep track of such things. And you need a work permit."

He glowered.

So I offered him an option. I said, "Why don't you come back to the States with me? You don't want to wait here for the police to come after you. If you do that, they'll arrest you, and then you'll probably spend time in jail before being deported.

Why wait for that? You aren't hidden here. I found you and other people could, too." I looked at him. "Maybe you think Vasily Rostov is searching for you in the Adirondacks. Don't worry. He hasn't been seen recently, and I'm told that he probably went back to Russia. He didn't testify against you before he left. The official records of the shooting on the horse trail say that he was shot by 'a person or persons unknown.' So you're not a wanted man in the U. S. You'll be wanted here, though, if you don't leave soon. So why not go back home with me? I could even give you a ride."

He glowered again. But I had tried.

So I went to the Canadian authorities and reported him as an illegal immigrant. I knew he wouldn't leave Canada without being pushed.

While waiting for the Canadian government to get itself together and deport Reilly, I stayed at the Cozy Corner motel in Gananoque. Nobody knew I was there, or so I thought. I wasn't expecting visitors, and I wasn't prepared for them. When I entered Canada, the customs officer asked whether I had a firearm. I told him I did not. Unfortunately, that was a truthful answer.

* * *

Linda was feeling a bit neglected. Saranac Lake was too far from Gananoque for me to commute, and I needed to stay in Canada to watch Reilly. Linda had plenty to do to keep busy—teaching school, taking care of William, cooking, housekeeping—but she wanted to see me and I wanted to see her. I called her when I could, but the Canadian telephone company charged me an arm and a leg for long distance, and that expense wasn't covered by my government budget. I promised Linda that I would return to Saranac as soon as possible.

As I was taking a short nap, there was a knock on my door. I was cautious. So I opened the door only a few inches.

"Hastings! What are you doing here?"

"I tracked you down, Joseph. Tracked you to your lair."

"How did you find me?"

"I'm a professional."

I thought. "Linda. She's incapable of resisting your charms."

"Would that it were so."

I invited him in. Hastings took the only chair and said, "Ah, the accommodations of a government employee." The motel was modest. I sat on the bed.

I reminded him, "You haven't told me why you're here."

He said, "I thought perhaps you might have Bill Reilly in your sights."

"No, I just like the exotic food. A weakness for poutine."

"What?"

"Never mind." He looked puzzled, so I relented. "Cheese curds and French fries with gravy, a Canadian specialty. It's in the same general food group as bubble and squeak, bangers and mash, and toad in the hole. Nutritious."

"What would an American know about bubble and squeak?"

"I'm a man of the world…Actually, my father was stationed in England during the war, waiting for D-Day. He told stories."

"You may make an intelligence operative yet. Any man willing to endure British home-cooking clearly has the courage for hazardous duty." Hastings pulled out a pack of Senior Service cigarettes. "I'm here because you're here and because I'm sure you're here because Reilly is."

"You know that he's here?"

"No, but you do."

"Why do you need him?"

"I've told you." Hastings said, "I think he killed Kuznetsov."

"No you don't. You want to silence him."

Hastings was all innocence. "Why would I want to do that?"

"Because he knows something."

"Has Rabbit Maranville told you what that is?"

The question surprised me. I thought it was an odd thing for him to say. The question suggested that Rabbit might have more information than I did. But I concluded that Hastings was probing, so I evaded it. I changed the subject. "Does Bill Reilly make sense to you?"

"What do you mean?"

"What's his motivation? Why did he pass secrets to your employers?"

"Ideology, I assume. He's probably a good Communist or an enthusiastic fellow traveler."

I didn't buy it. "I don't see any evidence of that."

"You know he's active in the Progressive Labor Party."

"No I don't. I know that he has some PL friends, but I don't know that he's really been active. It doesn't make sense to me. He's a techie, not a dreamer. I think maybe he was being paid by your employers."

"If he was, they haven't shared that information with me. All I know from Moscow is that he was an asset developed by Kuznetsov." Hastings was playing the employee, ill-informed by management. Maybe that was true.

"But why did he cooperate? Are you sure he wasn't paid?"

"I suppose he could have been. It could even have been done without Moscow's knowledge. Colonel Kuznetsov had a discretionary budget, not a large one, but enough." Hastings paused. "Maybe money wasn't needed. Marxism can be very attractive."

"Not to Bill Reilly. He's not a philosopher. He's a techie." Then I decided to tell Hastings more. "Langley is very good at gathering information. We know what Reilly reads. He doesn't know beans about Marx or Marcuse or Regis Debray. He reads *Playboy*."

"Lust is not incompatible with a socialist conscience."

"If you say so. He also reads *Popular Science*. He's a draftsman. He goes to church at Reverend Mordecai's storefront. He's not a bomb thrower. He carries around Mao's *Little Red Book* and he's probably memorized a few phrases, but it's a pose. That's about it. He isn't serious. So why would he want to take the risk of being a spy?"

"What do you care about his motivation? You caught him passing documents. He's guilty. So nail him."

"I thought a good agent was supposed to try to understand the adversary so that you can anticipate his moves and know where he's vulnerable."

"You've been reading too many romantic novels. Cassius Clay didn't need to know Henry Cooper's motivation, all he needed to know was that Cooper is a bleeder. Aim for the cheekbones and the eyebrows."

I said, "You are a man of many parts."

"If you know about bubble and squeak, you should certainly know about Henry Cooper."

"Do you want coffee?" I was trying to distract him by playing the host. I was unsuccessful.

"No, where's Reilly?"

"Right now, I'm not sure. He was working at Blackwell's Marina at the foot of River Street, but I've reported to Canadian Immigration that he crossed the border illegally. I don't think he's in custody, at least not yet, but I hope he will be."

"He'll do a runner."

I questioned that. "Does he have a place to go?"

"Family?"

I decided to give him the benefit of the CIA's research. Rabbit would not have approved. "Not much. Parents in Syracuse. That's not a place to hide."

"Girlfriend?"

"Not that I've seen any sign of."

"What does he do for amusement?"

"Langley says he's been known to take a drink, but I don't think he's a lush."

We had reached an impasse. The conversation stalled, so I turned to that old reliable, the weather. Compared to the temperatures in Saranac Lake, the weather in Gananoque was mild, about in the mid-40s, and Hastings wasn't wearing an overcoat, but he had on a handsome tweed jacket that looked like it might be bullet-proof. The jacket was a tan and heather color, had five buttons up the front and a high collar, and the tweed was thick enough to stand up on its own.

"Hastings, how many sheep did it take to produce that jacket?"

"I wouldn't know, lad. I'm not a shepherd nor a weaver. I just wear the thing. But I can tell you that it's well-made. It has taken some knocking about."

"What sort of jacket is it? It's an unusual design."

"It's what is known in my homeland as 'the keeper's jacket.'"

"Who is the keeper? What does he keep?"

Hastings paused. "Certainly not the Ten Commandments."

I laughed.

Then Hastings said, "The keeper usually kept game, as in 'gamekeeper,' as in Lady Chatterley's lover. But sometimes the keeper kept the dogs for the fox hunt."

I was quick. "To acquire that jacket, which did you sleep with, Lady Chatterley or the dogs?"

"Very droll. Very droll."

I quit while I was ahead and returned to pursuit of Reilly.

"Why are we concentrating on Reilly? He was in a business relationship with Kuznetsov, we know that. But so what? As far as we know, the business was entirely satisfactory, for both of them—Kuznetsov was getting information and Reilly was getting money. Why cut that off? I think we should be looking for a different killer."

"Perhaps."

"Why are you so sure that Reilly did it? I think you have more information."

"That is, of course, always a possibility. And I could say the same of you."

That was pretty much the end of the conversation. I said, "Anyhow, I like the keeper's jacket."

* * *

The next day, while Reilly was at Blackwell's Marina painting a skiff, a drop of paint fell onto a varnished seat and he bent over quickly to wipe it up. As he bent, he heard something hit the side of the building just beyond the boat. He looked up, saw a bullet hole at the level where his head had been, and then fell over sideways as a second bullet tore a hole in the skiff. Neither of those movements was intended as an evasive maneuver, but they probably saved his life. It's possible that the shooter was missing on purpose—the shots could have been a warning—but this didn't seem like the most obvious explanation.

Other people were at the marina at the time, eyewitnesses, and I interviewed them. They told me that it sounded like a rifle half a block away. They couldn't see where the shooter was. A building up the hill could have hidden someone, but the windows in the building were at least a hundred yards from the skiff. An ambitious shot. A rifle with a telescopic sight? Maybe.

If the shots were fired by Hastings, he wasn't as lethal as had been advertised, and he denied that it was his work. I'm not expressing a judgment on whether the denial was true or false. No one had seen him nearby, at least no one I could find. It was possible that the Soviets had sent someone to replace Rostov and take out Reilly. But, if that was the case, it had to mean both that they had lost confidence in Hastings—but why?—and that Reilly knew something very important—but what? I didn't have the answers. I had to find them.

According to the witnesses, as soon as Reilly saw the bullet holes, he ran down to the dock and jumped into a big, powerful speedboat he had worked on earlier. It was either a Hacker Craft or a Gar Wood, I don't remember which, probably from the 1930s. During Prohibition there was lively traffic here ferrying whiskey across the river from Canada to the States in boats like the one Reilly stole. No one could catch it.

The boat was fast, but easy to track and identify. The marina had photos and all the numbers and specs. I found it the next day moored on Dark Island, a mass of rock in the middle of the St. Lawrence topped by a chateau built at the turn of the century by the Singer sewing machine family. The property was unoccupied.

I enlisted the customs and immigration cops, but there was

a brief argument about jurisdiction. The boat was owned by a Canadian and had been stolen in Canada, but Dark Island is a few yards south of Canada, just on the US side of the border, which runs along the middle of the river. After asserting their powers, the authorities of the two nations decided to cooperate. Together they provided ten officers to search the place. It wasn't easy. The island has plenty of big rocks to hide behind, the castle has twenty-eight bedrooms, and there were rumored to be secret panels that led to hiding places. That may have been hooey, but the immigration cops had fun looking for them. The bottom line was that Reilly wasn't there. The boat was found, but he wasn't.

We later discovered that he took a rowboat from the boathouse on the island. Straight across from there, on the US mainland, the home of a woman known as Mary Ocean sits on top of a large rock ledge. Her house is cantilevered out over the river, and from Dark Island it looks like a ship. She's an artist and an interesting character. Maybe a retired bootlegger. Paints very big chickens and an occasional gorilla. She may have helped Reilly escape. When I asked her whether she had seen him, she launched into an irrelevant story about seeing a bear on the stairway in her house. I think she understood the question. In any event, Reilly was gone.

I returned to Gananoque to pick up my clothes and check out of the motel. Hastings was waiting for me.

He said, "I see you've returned empty-handed."

I replied, "And what fish have you caught?"

"Yes, we must do better. He's a bad man."

"I'm not so sure that he's the man I should be looking for."

"If he isn't guilty, why's he running?"

"He's running because somebody's shooting at him. Seems like a pretty good reason."

Chapter Eleven

Three days later I had news for Linda.

"Hastings found him. Reverend Mordecai was the key once again. They're really not very clever. Every time Reilly shows up at Mordecai's door, the Rev starts buying extra groceries. So Hastings gave ten bucks to the checkout boy at the Piggly Wiggly and that buys a list of the purchases for the week. Then Mordecai leads you to him. Reilly's hiding now at a house in Indian Lake. I suppose I should stop by and have another conversation with him, but I'm not sure what that would accomplish. He isn't talking."

She asked the obvious question. "Why not just arrest him and prosecute him for passing secrets?"

"That would be more expensive than it's worth. Langley thinks Reilly is small potatoes. I'm not sure that the information he gave Kuznetsov was even very secret. The map of the mine tunnels sure wasn't. You found essentially the same thing in the university archives."

"Is Hastings going to take another shot at him?"

I doubted it. "I'm not at all sure that Hastings wants to kill him."

She batted it back. "Well, somebody certainly shot at Reilly in Gananoque."

"Yeah, but he missed. That's not consistent with Hastings's reputation."

"Well, then why's Hastings here? And why's he tracking Reilly?"

"Maybe he was sent here to keep an eye on me. When he first got here, Moscow seemed to think I had killed Kuznetsov. Or so they said."

"But now the focus has turned to Reilly." Then Linda volunteered for service. "Maybe I should talk to him."

"Why?"

"Maybe he'd be more willing to talk to me. Maybe I'd be less threatening. And a man talks to a woman differently than he talks to another man. Haven't you ever noticed that?"

"Well, sometimes. But a man and a woman can talk professionally, dispassionately." I rumpled her hair.

Linda did one of her halfway smiles. "Yes. Or not."

"Wait a minute. What does that mean? What kind of a meeting are you going to have with him?"

"Oh, don't be silly." Linda held up both hands, palms out. "What do we have to lose?"

So Linda arranged to talk with Bill Reilly.

* * *

I have only her version of their conversation, not his, but I'm certain that she's an entirely reliable witness. She met him at a bench overlooking the lake in the municipal park at Tupper. There was a light breeze off the water. The sun warmed them. She remembered the weather that day and thought that it might have influenced the conversation. When they began, the sky was clear, a strong blue with a touch of green. But as the conversation went on, clouds gathered and the air turned cold.

"Do you have a girlfriend, Bill?"

"No."

"Why not?"

"Why do you want to know? Do you want to be my girlfriend?"

"I'm just curious. I haven't seen you with any girls, and I haven't heard of any girlfriend. Are you gay?" She used the halfway smile again.

"No."

"Some of the other girls and I were talking about it."

"Talking about me?"

"Yes, that's right."

"Why?"

"Well, you're a handsome young guy, a college graduate, you appear to be healthy, why not? Girls would be interested."

"They don't tell me that."

"I just did."

Bill turned on the bench and looked over at the baseball diamond. "What are women looking for in a man?"

"That's a good question."

"Do they just want the stuff you said, a healthy college graduate, or do they want good looks, romance, excitement?"

"You don't need to worry about the good looks. You're just fine. But I don't think the guy being good looking has much to do with it. I guess most women like romance, excitement."

"Okay."

"Are you an exciting guy, Bill?"

"Sometimes." Bill turned back toward Linda and met her eyes. "You don't know everything about me."

"Give me an example."

"I have a secret."

"Oh, I love secrets. They're exciting."

"Yeah."

"What is it?"

"I can't say."

"Well, then, it isn't much use, is it?"

Bill looked away again. He put on a wool watch cap, zipped his windbreaker higher on his neck, and took a deep breath. "Do you remember that dead body found at Axton Landing?"

"Sure, it was in the newspapers."

"Well, I saw that man meeting with another guy."

"So what?" Linda asked, "Why shouldn't he?"

"It was peculiar and suspicious. I don't think they wanted to be seen." Bill shifted uncomfortably on the bench. "The man who was killed was a Russian. I don't think that's been in the newspapers."

"You're well-informed."

"On this I am. You bet."

"How do you know the man you saw was the one killed at Axton? And how do you know he was Russian?"

"Captain Boudreau told me. I met with the man when I thought he was Dr. Lien. Boudreau told me that he was a Russian."

"Who was the other guy?"

"I think he was an Air Force officer. Later I saw him in uniform."

Now Linda pressed the questioning quickly, giving Reilly less time to consider his answers. "How did you do that?"

"I followed him."

"Where?"

"Do you know the old steamboat landing on Utowanna Lake?"

"Utowanna is one of the lakes in the Eckford chain, isn't it?"

"Yeah, that's right. Blue Mountain Lake, then Eagle Lake, then Utowanna."

"What were the men doing there?"

"Nothing. Talking. Just standing by the access to the Marion River carry. They didn't have a boat. I couldn't see any reason why they were there, except to meet."

"What were you doing there?"

"I was camping on Utowanna, near the steamboat landing. I go there often."

She kept the questions coming. "How'd you happen to see them?"

"I'd taken my canoe out of the water across from the landing and I was getting ready to go home. There they were, standing next to two cars parked just off the road."

"You didn't go up to them?"

"No, I didn't want them to see me."

"You said you followed the other guy."

"Yeah, I did. They only talked for a couple of minutes more after I first saw them, maybe three or four minutes. Then they got into the two cars and the Russian drove southwest, in the direction of Inlet and Old Forge, and the other guy drove toward Blue Mountain Lake. I padlocked my canoe to a tree and then followed in my truck. The guy went to the village and stopped at Potters resort. I parked across the street. I wanted to find out who he was."

Linda buttered him up. "This is very cool. So what did you do?"

"I waited outside Potters for ten or fifteen minutes but he didn't come out, so I decided to go in and look for him. He wasn't in the lobby. They have guest rooms in the main lodge and he must have been in one of them. So I decided to have a cup of coffee and watch for him. After a few more minutes, he showed up in the lobby, went to the registration desk, and paid his bill. But he was dressed differently. Before, he was wearing a red and black checked shirt, what some people call a buffalo plaid, but now he was in a blue Air Force uniform."

"Are you sure it was the same man?"

"Absolutely. I got a good look at him at Utowanna, and he was only about six feet away from me at Potters."

Linda did her job. "What does he look like?"

"He's tall, thin, with black wavy hair, starting to go grey, maybe about fifty years old. When I first saw Joe Boudreau at the Long Lake Hotel, wearing the same kind of uniform, I thought he might be connected with this guy, but I guess he isn't."

"No, I don't think so. What was the man's rank?"

"I don't know all of the military insignia, decorations, and medals. He had some colored ribbons on his chest. On his shoulder, where Boudreau has captain's bars (I recognize those), this man had an eagle."

"An eagle standing up?"

"No, of course not, a flat eagle, about the size of captain's bars."

"Do you think this could be the person who killed the Russian?"

"Sure, why not?"

"Could you identify him if you saw him again?"

"Sure."

"Who knows that?"

"Maybe the person who was shooting at me. But I haven't told anyone."

Linda pressed it. "Could you identify the man from a photograph?"

"Probably, but I'm not going to. I'm too visible already. I'm smart enough to know when it's time to disappear."

"Yeah, but you haven't disappeared. You need someone to protect you. Hastings knows where you are."

"Hastings is scary." Reilly looked at the baseball diamond again, then out at the lake.

"Hastings is worse than scary."

"Can I move in with you?"

Linda was surprised. She probably shouldn't have been. "No. You can't. I have a son to protect. I have to keep him safe."

"What should I do?"

"I think you should tell your story to Joe Boudreau."

"He'll have me arrested."

"I don't think so, and anyway that's probably better than what Hastings would do to you."

Reilly stood and walked away.

* * *

So Linda delivered the goods. Reilly contacted me the next day and told me the same things he had told her. Then Linda and I tried to figure out what to make of it. We were in her kitchen drinking coffee, with four-year-old William sipping on a glass of milk and looking at a Richard Scarry book. One advantage of William's age was that he didn't understand our conversations. At least not yet.

I spoke first. "This smells wrong. Bill Reilly says that he just happened to be camping at Utowanna Lake and so he just happened to see Kuznetsov and another man. Do you believe that? It seems pretty convenient. Isn't it more likely that Reilly is inventing the other man, an Air Force officer, in order to have someone to blame for Kuznetsov's killing, a suspect other than himself?"

"That could be. But surely you should report Reilly's story to Rabbit to see what he thinks. Maybe Langley knows something about what was going on. And we might be able to confirm whether Potters had a guest who fit the description Reilly gave us. A high-ranking Air Force officer, in uniform, would be pretty conspicuous."

"Okay. Reilly said the officer had the eagle, right?"

Linda nodded. "That means he's a colonel, doesn't it?"

"Yeah, a full colonel. What we call a 'bird colonel' as opposed to a 'light colonel'."

"Would a colonel have design details for the TFX?"

"He might. It depends on what his job is. But, even if Reilly is telling the truth, we don't know for sure that the guy was really an officer. He could have just been a man wearing a uniform."

"Why would the man do that?"

"Maybe to throw us off, to put us on the wrong track."

"Okay, but why would he permit himself to be seen with Kuznetsov in the first place? It wasn't a very secret meeting. And what was he doing here? Are there Air Force people stationed at Tahawus?"

I fidgeted with my coffee cup. "No, I'm sure there aren't. I would know if we had officers there."

Linda paused and offered me an oatmeal raisin cookie. I accepted. William got one too. She said, "So where would a colonel who knew details about the TFX be likely to work?"

"Probably at the Pentagon, or maybe around the factory that's building the plane."

"If he was working for the Russians, why come to the Adirondacks instead of meeting with them in Washington or Houston?"

"Maybe they thought they'd be less likely to be seen in the Adirondacks than in D.C. Or maybe the officer came because Kuznetsov was the agent in charge of the Soviet operation and he was here. Kuznetsov might have been eager to avoid D.C."

Linda said, "I don't know. What if they wanted to be seen here?"

It was my turn to be doubtful. "I don't think so. It was just their bad luck that Reilly was at Utowanna Lake."

"Unless." Linda paused. "Unless Kuznetsov knew that Reilly camped at Utowanna. But why would he want to be seen?"

"Yeah, that's pretty subtle. And pretty unlikely."

"As Reilly suggested, maybe the officer…"

I interrupted her. "Or bogus officer. Let's just call him the third man."

She shrugged. "Okay. Maybe the third man killed Kuznetsov."

"Yeah, maybe, but there's nothing in Reilly's account to suggest that. The two men parted, Kuznetsov drove in one direction and the third man in the other, toward Potters, where he checked out. It's significant, of course, that Reilly chose to follow the third man rather than Kuznetsov. That tells us he already knew who the Russian was but he didn't know the other guy. Reilly must have had dealings with Kuznetsov by that point. And we don't have any evidence that Kuznetsov and the third man ever met again."

She said, "But they could have."

"Yes, they could have. We also don't know where the third man was when Kuznetsov was killed, and it's going to be pretty hard to find that out if we don't know more about who he was."

"It's possible that he was another Soviet agent, maybe even one sent here to kill Kuznetsov."

"Or maybe he was Kuznetsov's boss. There are a lot of possibilities." I helped myself to another oatmeal raisin cookie. William was still looking at his book and didn't ask for another cookie.

Linda said, "You don't get fat."

"Maybe someday." I finished my cookie in two bites. "I wonder whether Hastings knows about the third man."

"Would he tell us?"

"Not unless he thought it was in his interest to tell us. But I could try to figure out whether he was surprised. For an experienced operative, Hastings isn't really a very good actor."

"Or maybe he's so good that he's persuaded you that he's not."

I laughed, "Well, we certainly unraveled all of that. Nobody is going to put anything over on us, by golly!"

It was chilly outside by that time, and the wind had picked up. William went to bed. I hugged Linda for warmth and with a sense of gratitude, but also for something to hold onto. And then we made love. I'll omit the details.

* * *

I suppose I should say how I felt about Linda—that's a part of the story. The truth is, I was still trying to figure out how I felt. I wasn't head-over-heels. I'm not a head-over-heels kind of guy. Am I a calculating person? Maybe. Certainly, I like to know the odds—I look for trouble ahead. My previous girlfriends had turned out to be short-term relationships, mostly because of a lack of commitment on both sides. Susan would have been nice, but she was rather dull. Rowena would have been great, probably, but she was beyond reach. I wasn't in her league.

They say that ducks "imprint" on their mates. It's a type of bonding. The process is not well-understood, but it's apparently more or less automatic. It's a very strong attachment. Some men and women mate as if they were imprinting. But I'm not a duck. I think it's human to be rational, contemplative.

There are too many divorces. I didn't want to add another one. Linda had already been divorced, and she didn't want to chance it again. We were both cautious, but I certainly liked her a lot. And, I was impressed by her and we had fun. She was affectionate and a good mother. I enjoyed her company. I could imagine spending my whole life with her, which seemed a real possibility, an attractive one.

I realized that I was getting a little older. Maybe it was time for me to start thinking about some longer-term decisions. So why was I hesitating? Simply caution, I think. Difficulty pulling the trigger.

I was in a dangerous job. Would I be putting her and her child in danger? Maybe. Would I sacrifice my life for her? Yes, definitely. I guess that's a pretty good measure of commitment.

When it comes right down to it, there are really only a few ways to say 'I love you,' none of them original, and the simplest are almost always the best. Linda and I exhausted the possibilities of the language, verbal and physical.

* * *

While I was taking a shower, Rabbit called. Linda answered.

When I got on, he said, "A woman answered the phone."

"Yes."

"Who was that?"

"Linda."

"Oh. Has she been cleared?"

"No."

"How much does she know?"

"Pretty much everything."

"Aren't you troubled by that?"

"No, not really. She hasn't seen any classified material. For that matter, neither have I. I stumbled on to a murder victim, and I'm trying to help the police. I'm just working to solve a puzzle." Rabbit knew it was more than that, but I gave him cover.

He said, "Look, we need to have a more extended discussion about this, sometime when she isn't in the room with you. You know the rules. If you violate them, be prepared to take the consequences. But I don't want to tie your hands. I know you're trying to do your job. For now, I have to trust your judgment. I don't have much alternative. I could take you off this matter, but your family connections in Saranac give you a big advantage for doing the job. If I had anyone better to put on it, I'd do it. But I don't. So it's your job, for now. But don't embarrass me."

Rabbit lived in the real world. There were regulations, and then there was getting the job done.

I said, "If you'd send one or two more men up here, Rabbit, I wouldn't have to rely on Linda."

"You seem to think the Agency has unlimited manpower and an unlimited budget. If you think that, you're wrong. And there are other priorities, some of them higher. There's a war in Vietnam and subversion here. We do the job with the resources we have available."

The truth is that I liked working with Linda, and I liked that arrangement better than having the CIA send another agent to

Saranac. I hoped they wouldn't. If the Agency decided to punish me for violating regulations, I would accept my punishment. I liked my job well enough, but I wasn't sure I wanted to do it forever. The Air Force wouldn't court-martial me—that would cause publicity about what my real job was. If the Agency decided to cut me loose, I wouldn't stay in the Air Force. To make a living, I could go to Wisconsin and work for my Uncle Vince in his canoe rental, guiding, and outfitter business. That was my summer job during my last two years of high school and my first two years of college, leading trips on the Flambeau, the Namekagon, and the Couderay. Nice rivers. I liked the work and Vince likes me. Hayward is a good town, something like Saranac Lake. Linda would be comfortable there.

But what Rabbit then told me was a game-changer. The Soviets had design details for the TFX that could not have come from Tahawus. The lab at the titanium mine didn't have access to those specs, and Reilly couldn't have seen them or been able to get his hands on them. This didn't change the fact that he had passed classified information, but it meant there had to be another spy, which made Reilly's story about the third man much more credible.

The CIA was investigating. Rabbit didn't yet tell me how they were doing it—maybe Linda's involvement stopped him from saying more—but I knew that he was working with Withrow Wren, the chief of counterintelligence, a legendary spy catcher.

Rabbit was, of course, very interested in what Bill Reilly had to say. As soon as he heard about the third man, he wanted me to come down to Langley to discuss it. We debated whether Reilly should be hauled down to D.C. to be questioned more systematically and intensively, and shown photographs of possible suspects. I recommended against it. Reilly had said that he would refuse to look at photos, and I thought that Linda and I already had the useful information.

I also worried about Hastings's reaction. I had decided not to tell him about the third man because he would surely have alerted Moscow so that they could "exfiltrate" their agent (as we say in the biz). If we could identify the third man, we would want to keep our hands on him at least until we determined how much harm he had done. Rabbit accepted this reasoning, but summoned me to Langley for further discussion.

A day later, when I walked into Rabbit's office, he was writing standing up. In addition to his sitting-down desk, he had an old one designed for use while sitting on a high stool, like Bob Cratchit's desk in *A Christmas Carol*. But Rabbit dispensed with the stool and just stood. The desk looked out of place in a sleek modern office building. It was a dark red color, probably the result of buttermilk stain, a mixture of the milk and blood of cows. That seemed peculiarly appropriate at the CIA. The stain gives pine or poplar a color that in low light might look like mahogany or cherry, but the fluorescent bulbs in Rabbit's office didn't permit that mistake. The joinery of the desk made clear that it was rustic.

I asked, "Why are you standing?"

"Back pain. Better when I'm straight."

"Always good to be straight."

"Really?"

It was a corner office. There was an American flag on a pole standing by the windows, getting light from both north and east. Rabbit paced the room as he talked, but he kept his eyes on the flag. He walked in a set pattern, which was repeated. It was a fascinating performance. When his steps put the flag beyond his line of sight, he'd do a smart about-face and head back toward it. He'd obviously done this before, and he was good at it. It was distracting, like someone playing with a pencil. What was the point of it? A test of my concentration? I didn't think so. It was just an odd habit, a quirk, something like writing his name with the stem of his pipe. His mind needed to do more than one thing at a time.

He told me that Wren had planted several pieces of slightly wrong TFX design data. They weren't greatly wrong, just a small detail off here and there. The pieces were planted systematically in relevant places within the Pentagon and in the companies working on the plane. When one of these erroneous details showed up in Moscow, as reported by our asset there, we would know where it had come from. This had to be done very carefully and subtly because the other side would be watching for it. The error had to look right; it had to be plausible.

Rabbit recruited Paul Nitze, the Secretary of the Navy, to help with the plan. The TFX was to be a fighter plane used by both the Air Force and the Navy, so the Navy part of the project was within Nitze's jurisdiction. He was a smooth operator, well-tailored, small, with a full head of white hair neatly combed, a gentleman. Dapper but serious. Rabbit and Nitze were both from Chicago. Before wartime service in the OSS, Rabbit practiced law in Chicago, and the two of them moved in the same social circles. Rabbit trusted Nitze and they worked well together. The old boys' club.

* * *

While the experts at Langley devised credible errors in the design specs and worked out where and how to plant them, I was in the Adirondacks pursuing Reilly's story. The obvious place to start was at Potter's, where someone other than Reilly might have seen the third man.

Potter's was doing a good business. The parking in front of the inn was full, so I put my car near the tennis courts overlooking the lake. There was a stiff breeze, a chop on the water, and no tennis that day. I'd made an appointment with Mr. Potter and I went straight to his office.

I showed him my Air Force ID. He said, "I know a good many Boudreaus."

"All of them are my kin."

"A good, big family."

"Yes to both. And thank you." He offered his hand and I shook it. "Mr. Potter, you had a guest recently who may or may not have been an Air Force officer."

"Well, we get men here from Griffiss from time to time, taking a break. They're welcome, of course, but I wish they wouldn't send their fighter jets screaming over here. Jolts the customers out of bed and disturbs the fish."

"The person who can do the most about that is the Congressman. Call him or write him."

"Will do. Now, who is the man you're interested in?"

"That's what I'm trying to find out. He would have been here about a month ago, I believe. Do you remember anyone in uniform?"

"Let me check our guest register and see if that triggers anything."

He went to the desk, got the register, brought it back to his office, and flipped through it, page by page. "About a month ago, you said. There's a name here that I remember, Arthur Armstrong. Tall man, dark hair, sharp features. I think he might be the one."

"Did you see him in uniform?

"No, not that I recall."

"What makes you think he was Air Force?"

"I'm not sure, but that just seems right."

"How old was he?"

"Maybe early fifties. Not young."

"Why do you remember him?"

"I checked him in. His suitcase had the initials AAA, so I asked him whether it stood for 'American Automobile Association.' He said no, that those were his initials, which made sense when I got his name, Arthur Armstrong. He also said he considered using AA as his monogram but then he thought it might be taken as meaning Alcoholics Anonymous."

"Did he pay with a credit card?"

"Let me look." He consulted another record, and said, "No, he paid cash."

"How much was his bill?"

"$256. He was here three nights and ate two dinners."

"Do many customers pay bills of that size with cash?"

"No, not many. But some do."

"Is there anything else you can tell me about him?"

"I don't think so. All I remember for sure is the AAA on his suitcase."

"Thank you very much, Mr. Potter. This is helpful."

"Any time. Give my regards to your cousins."

Chapter Twelve

I reported to Rabbit. He told me that one of the men on Wren's list was named Alfred Adams. Then he checked further and found that the man's full name was Alfred Aldrich Adams. He was an Air Force colonel. Reilly's story was sounding better all the time.

Adams was a lawyer. He worked in the office of the Air Force general counsel, a part of the staff of the Secretary, and was assigned to legislative liaison, working on the congressional hearings about the TFX. There was conflict between two contractors, Boeing and General Dynamics, and both had congressmen advocating their interests. Colonel Adams had access to design details because the design was what they were fighting about.

Rabbit told me I would not be involved in the investigation of Colonel Adams. That would be handled by Langley. But he said I needed to know about Adams for whatever bearing it might have on Reilly, Kuznetsov, and Hastings. I was not to muck about in it unless Adams showed up in the Adirondacks again. Rabbit was unusually kind and solicitous in the telephone call when he delivered this message. Ordinarily he was very businesslike — not brusque, exactly, but businesslike. On this call, however, he said he wanted to assure me that I had his trust, that he valued my work, and that this compartmentalization was just the way the CIA did business. I was their North Country man. I accepted that.

So I went back to the Axton file. We still didn't know who had killed Kuznetsov, or why, and it was my job to find out. We were less concerned about Soviet protests. If they wanted to put spies on our territory, they could take their chances, but the Axton killing was a murder that took place on our soil, a murder of a foreign national, and it had national security implications. (As I thought this, however, I preferred not to consider the Rostov complication.)

In the course of the investigation, I had acquired two partners. One was Linda. I've already talked about that. The other partner, Hastings, just sort of happened. I didn't exactly choose him. He was there and our interests coincided, at least some of the time. Did I trust him? Certainly not. Did I like him? Well, he had his moments. He had saved my life, after all. (I'm not sure why he did that, but I think he was happy to get rid of Rostov, who may have been a competitor for the Kremlin's favor, or there may have been an old grievance, a pretty serious one.) Hastings clearly knew a lot more about the spy business than I did, and he would be a very valuable ally if I could trust him, but we worked for different people, people who didn't like each other.

In any event, I saw Hastings frequently—there was no avoiding it. In fact, I didn't see Linda as much as I would have liked, and I saw Hastings more often than I shaved (and I had to look like a clean-shaven Air Force officer, not a hippie). We set up a regular meeting place, a table in a corner at the back of the Full Moon. We called it the gangster table—we each had our back to a wall, with a clear view of the front door, so anyone coming at us would have to come head on. No one was going to surprise us. It was a joke, a small one, but we enjoyed it. Hastings, I think, chose that sort of seating by instinct.

I tried to keep the information about Colonel Adams away from Hastings, but that was difficult to do. Somehow he found out that I had been to Blue Mountain Lake to ask questions at Potters. He may have tailed me (he was good at that) or he may have had paid informants. He passed out money liberally. In any event, Hastings went to Blue and had his own conversation with Mr. Potter, who told him that I had been asking questions about an Air Force Colonel, Arthur Armstrong. That made it all too clear to Hastings. If Adams was working for the Ruskies (and he was), they knew it and would have no trouble equating Colonel Adams and Colonel Armstrong. This was bad not only because the Soviets might help Adams escape, but because it prevented us from trying to persuade (or compel) Adams to become a double agent so we could feed disinformation to the opposition. Had Hastings not been onto it, that would have been an attractive possibility.

The next time I saw Hastings at the gangster table, he simply said, "I understand you're interested in an Air Force colonel."

I tried to keep a poker face. "We have a lot of them. Is one of them working for you?"

He said, "The law of probabilities suggests that if you have enough colonels and there's enough money on the table, one of the colonels will take the money. But that's a long way from having proof."

I knew he liked Linda. "This isn't getting us anywhere. Do I need to bring Linda in to charm you?"

"I wish you would."

I laughed and said, "Why don't we just lay our cards on the table?"

"Jolly good. You first."

"Okay. What do you know?"

"That wasn't what I had in mind." He lowered his voice. "But obviously we're both thinking of the same person, an Air Force colonel who conspicuously puts his initials on his luggage and parades around in his uniform, at least part of the time. Either not terribly bright or absurdly arrogant, which may be the same thing."

I said, "Unless someone is trying to frame Colonel Adams." Since the Soviets already knew about Adams—he was their agent—no further harm could be done by naming him.

At that point there was a large crash because a waitress dropped an armload of dishes. Several broke. A bit of spaghetti with sauce bolognese ended up on Hastings's tan suede desert boots. He was annoyed. I hoped it would distract him, but it didn't. He said, "Too subtle, too subtle—your thesis, that is, not the broken crockery."

So I replied. "Adams was seen. I think he could be identified."

"Why have you not done it then?"

I looked at him. I thought he was playing dumb. Then I said, "Reilly."

"What about Reilly?"

"You really don't know? Reilly saw him."

"But, dear boy, he wasn't the only one. Potter could identify Adams." Hastings was back to his most British manner.

"Yes, but Reilly saw him with Kuznetsov. Potter didn't." I was pleased that he really was surprised because that suggested that Hastings probably wasn't the person who shot at Reilly.

"Aha…. I see. I see. The light begins to dawn."

"You really didn't know?"

"No. I see that I should have. And I see what it suggests to you."

"And what would that be?" I asked.

Hastings looked at the floor. "It suggests that Adams is the spy you were looking for, not Reilly."

"Ah. Then who killed Kuznetsov?"

He paused and looked sternly at me. "You think Adams did it, not Reilly."

"Could be, " I said.

"I don't believe so." He continued to stare at me, hard. "Why would Adams do that?"

"For the same reason that Reilly would, I suppose. They argued about control, or he wasn't being paid enough, or Kuznetsov threatened him. You know better than I why spies have a falling out."

He said, "Think about it." I asked him more questions, but his answer to every one of them was the same, "Think about it." So I did.

Later, Linda and I talked once again. We considered whether there was competition between Reilly and Adams, and whether Kuznetsov was playing one of them off against the other. According to Reilly's story, he didn't know Adams existed until he saw him with Kuznetsov at Utowanna. But I thought that story was improbable. On the other hand, improbable things happen.

Linda pointed out that if Reilly wanted to make up a story about seeing the two men together, he would have picked a place for that to happen that was more likely than Utowanna Lake. So maybe it was the truth. But I had seen Reilly put microfilm in the dead drop. That was a fact. There was no evidence that Adams passed anything, not even water, as we say in the trade. It wasn't a crime to be a guest at Potters and it wasn't even a crime to talk to a Russian (if, indeed, it was true that he had). And if Adams was a spy, why would he take the risk of being seen in the Adirondacks? Perhaps Kuznetsov drew him into the open. Perhaps Kuznetsov demanded the meeting. Maybe it was the safest way to exchange information, better than the telephone or putting it in writing.

But one man didn't need to be both the spy and the killer. It was possible, of course, that one was the spy and the other killed Kuznetsov. But why? And what about Rostov or Hastings as suspects? There were a lot of possibilities and little hard evidence. And Hastings told me to think about it. At this point I was very confused and depressed and about ready to pack it in.

* * *

And then there was another development, an important one. One of the false design specs planted by the CIA had turned up. It was the one put in the Office of the Secretary of the Air Force. It could have migrated from there to another agency and then from the other place to Moscow, but the place to start looking for the mole was in the Secretary's staff, a large office with hundreds of employees, both military and civilian, including Colonel Adams. Did he have access to the data? The answer to that question, I was told, was that his duties did not require him to have it. That was a careful answer, one providing reason to investigate, but not proof. This is the sort of thing that keeps investigators in business.

The first thing to nail down was whether the phony piece of data had been given to the general counsel's office, where Adams worked. (In the military way of doing things, every person, place, or thing is referred to by initials, so the office is called

SAFGC, which stands for Secretary of the Air Force General Counsel. It's sometimes pronounced "saf-gick"—not very dignified.) Wren and his troops handled that part of the investigation. I was in the Adirondacks while that was going on and I don't know the details, but they concluded that the design spec used as the marker had indeed gone to SAFGC. Where it went within that office was less clear. About fifteen lawyers worked there, but Adams certainly had access to the data. He could have seen it while working on the congressional hearings.

Meanwhile, Linda and I were still pursuing Reilly. Once again, she did the crucial work. She softened him up. (He liked her better. Everybody liked Linda better.) This time Linda wore a wire, so we have a transcript:

She said, "Bill, I think you'll be better off if you cooperate on identifying the guy you saw with Kuznetsov. Right now, you're the only person they know of who is connected to Kuznetsov. You were seen putting microfilm at the cemetery and he picked it up. They don't have any other link or tie to him. You're it. That makes you the prime suspect as his murderer. You'd be better off if another guy might have done it."

"I know that. I'm not dumb. But I don't want to get involved."

"You're already involved. That's why they're investigating the hell out of you. They're going to pin it on you."

"Is your boyfriend, Joe Boudreau, going to do that to me?"

"Joe's a good guy, Bill. He's an Adirondack guy just like you. He likes the woods and the water, just the way you do. You could get along with him. He'll give you an even break."

"I don't know. I'll think about it."

"Don't think too long, Bill. You're risking your neck. You need to give them someone else to focus on." Then you can hear on the recording that she lowered her voice. "To convict you of a crime, they have to prove you guilty beyond a reasonable doubt. If there's another suspect, how can they do that? How can there not be doubt? But if you're the only possibility, then it looks like it must have been you."

"Maybe you're right." And again he promised to think about it.

The next day Reilly decided to cooperate — that is, to identify the man he saw with Kuznetsov and at Potter's.

* * *

Since Wren and Rabbit now believed that Colonel Adams was, in fact, the third man, Reilly needed to go to D.C. to pick him out of a lineup. As a military officer, Adams could have been ordered to go to the Adirondacks, but if we had done that he would have known what was up, and then there would have been a real danger that he would run for it. Without Reilly's identification of him, we didn't yet have sufficient grounds for putting Adams under arrest, so I had to persuade Reilly to accept an all-expenses-paid trip to D.C. We put him up at a good hotel, at taxpayer expense. I got to go along.

Transporting Reilly was tricky. Because we wanted his cooperation and he wasn't under arrest, not yet, we couldn't use handcuffs. We were calling him a "voluntary witness", and handcuffs would certainly have been inconsistent with that. So I "accompanied" him. I kept him close to me and had my eyes on him. This was easy enough in the cars, in the airports, and on the plane. From Griffiss Air Force Base, just twenty miles or so from the southwest boundary of the Adirondack Park, we took a military flight to Andrews AFB, near the District. Military transportation was supposed to take us from there to the Pentagon, but the transport wasn't available—a situation captured by the acronym, SNAFU. So, after some confusion, we took a commercial bus. This was okay because the bus was confining enough, but when we reached the Pentagon we were let out into a large concourse on the ground floor that included shops, a drugstore, a big newsstand with papers from several cities, a large shoeshine parlor, and crowds of people. It became hard to keep track of Reilly without grabbing hold of him.

He wore his standard Adirondack gear—a flannel shirt, tan cotton pants, and a padded jacket—but, because we flew on an Air Force plane and because the meeting was at the Pentagon, I was wearing my uniform. When I saw the shoeshine parlor, I looked at my shoes. They were scuffed. I had to look sharp—I didn't want some general to reprimand me and make a note of my name, so I decided to get a shine. That was a mistake. While I was sitting on a raised chair so that my shoes were at a level that was comfortable for the man working on them, Reilly casually wandered away. When I discovered that he had gone, the shoes had not yet been buffed, but Reilly was more important. I jumped down from the chair, gave the man a large tip to compensate him for the damage to his professional pride, and went to look for Reilly. I found him at the newsstand, reading the headlines. I'm still not sure whether he was trying to ditch me or was just clueless.

I had to deliver him to an office on the C ring. Not only does the Pentagon have five sides, it also has five floors (plus some below-ground), and five concentric "rings" from the outside to the center of the building. So the C ring is in the middle, connecting all five of the sides. The arrangement is very logical, but it's certainly possible to get lost. What the logic doesn't tell you is where to find stairways or escalators to take you from one floor to another, or hallways to go from one ring to another. Some of the passages are closed off, probably for security reasons, and then you have to turn around and try again. I asked for directions several times and often received a variant of "you can't get there from here." It wasn't funny. You can walk many miles in that building, and it felt like we did, all the while looking at my watch. But we found the office.

An inter-agency working group had planned the investigative strategy. The group was chaired by Wren and it included Rabbit, Nitze, and Eugene Zukert, the Secretary of the Air Force. Care had been taken to keep the investigation quiet, but we needed to be sure that all of the SAFGC lawyers were available during Reilly's visit so Secretary Zukert arranged an "important meeting" with them for 11:00 a.m. on the day following Reilly's arrival.

But the first step was interrogation of Bill Reilly. Wren did the questioning. He was a handsome man in late middle-age with sandy hair thinning on top and a gentle manner. The manner was deceptive. Wren was from West Virginia but it must have been the fancy part, very near the Greenbriar. He knew which fork to use. His clothes were anonymous—they didn't attract attention. He looked comfortable. If he rode on a bus, none of the passengers would remember him.

He started with Utowanna Lake, the most improbable element in Reilly's story. Wren wanted to test Reilly's credibility.

"What were you doing at Utowanna Lake?"

"Camping."

"Just living there, in a tent?"

"No, I was only there for a couple of days, fishing."

"Do you do that often?"

"Yeah."

"How often?"

"When I feel like it." Reilly didn't know who Wren was and wasn't afraid of him. He should have been.

"Well, Mr. Reilly, you now know that Kuznetsov, a man you may have known as 'Dr. Lien', was in fact a colonel in the Soviet KGB. Is that correct?"

"I've been told that."

"And did Colonel Kuznetsov know you were camping at Utowanna Lake?"

"No, I don't think so."

"How did he happen to be there just at the time you were?"

"I don't know."

"Had you told him that you often camped there?"

"I don't remember telling him that."

"Didn't you in fact arrange to meet him at Utowanna?"

"No, I didn't."

"But you saw Kuznetsov at Utowanna?"

"Yes, I saw him talking with another man."

"And did you know who the other man was?"

"No."

"But you knew Kuznetsov, you recognized him?"

"Yes."

Sometimes Wren's questions came fast, and at other times there were long pauses between them. This didn't seem to bother Reilly, although it was probably intended to.

"So you had met with him before?"

"Well, I had lunch with Dr. Lien at the Long Lake Hotel."

"How many times?"

"I don't remember. It may have been more than once."

"Why did you meet with him?"

"He was interested in my work."

"Yes, he was. And you told him about it, didn't you?"

"I don't know."

"Yes you do. And you're also aware that you were observed putting microfilm with secret information into a dead drop at the Jewish cemetery and that the information was subsequently picked up by Kuznetsov. Right?"

Reilly didn't respond. So Wren continued:

"I'm trying to understand what was going on. If you were having lunch with Kuznetsov, or Dr. Lien, why didn't you just hand the microfilm to him then? Why did you use the drop in the cemetery?"

"Dr. Lien preferred to do it that way."

"Why would that be?"

"I don't know."

"Would it be because you might have been seen at the hotel handing materials to him and he, or you, didn't want that?"

"Is that why I'm here? I thought I was here to identify the man I saw talking to Dr. Lien."

Wren leaned back. He relaxed a bit. The people in the room breathed more easily.

Wren said, "And so you are. And so you are." He turned to Rabbit and asked, "Are we ready to proceed with that?"

Rabbit replied, "I think so. We can just go down the hall to the general counsel's office and get it organized."

Rabbit led the way. In the SAFGC conference room, the lawyers had been assembled for their meeting with Secretary Zukert. Some of the lawyers were military officers and some were not. Only a few of them wore the uniform. The room held twenty people comfortably. It was long and relatively narrow, with a large table in the middle, Air Force blue. One wall was all windows with a close view of the next ring. The other walls held some handsome color photographs of airplanes and missiles—not to everyone's taste, perhaps, but they told you where you were.

When we arrived at the door, Reilly and I were instructed to wait in the hall. Secretary Zukert was already in the room talking to the lawyers. Then Secretary Nitze arrived, and so did General Landon, the Deputy Chief of Staff of the Air Force. I'm told that the lawyers were startled and puzzled when Wren walked in followed by Nitze and Landon. Only a few of them recognized Wren, but many knew what Nitze looked like and most of them probably knew who Landon was. Then Rabbit summoned me with Bill Reilly in tow.

As we entered the room, Zukert said, "Gentlemen, we have an unusual piece of business today. I'm going to turn the meeting over to General Landon now."

Landon said, "Could a couple of you strong lawyers move the table out of the middle of the room? Just put it against the back wall, please. We're going to need space in the middle."

Most of the lawyers were eager to help, and the table and chairs were moved.

Then General Landon used his command voice: "Gentlemen, all of you lawyers please form a line, a single line in the middle of the room, facing the windows. Those of you who are in uniform will stand either at attention or at parade rest. Take your choice. Those of you who are civilians, please stand as straight as you can." He chuckled, slightly, or maybe it was a snarl.

There was a bit of confusion until the lawyers got themselves into a line. Then Landon said, "We're going to review the troops, in a manner of speaking."

Several of the lawyers were smiling. Landon said, "This is

not a joke. We regret that it's necessary, but it is." Some lawyers frowned.

Because the lawyers faced the windows, they were well-lighted. Reilly wouldn't have any trouble seeing them. And the sun was in their eyes, which was intimidating. I thought that this use of the windows was a bit cheesy, but sometimes the old, simple ways of doing things are the best.

Landon, Zukert, and Bill Reilly went to the left end of the line. Reilly had been told, both by me and by Wren, what he was to do. The three of them proceeded slowly along the line, looking at each man in turn. Landon first, then Zukert, then Reilly. When they reached the end of the line, they stopped. Zukert and Landon nodded at Reilly, who turned and walked back along the line until he reached Adams and put his hand on Adams's shoulder. Nobody spoke. How many seconds passed? It seemed a long time. Everyone tried not to look at Colonel Adams, but even without staring we could see the beads of sweat on his face. Finally, General Landon said, "Colonel Adams, come with me. You may consider that an order." Then Landon, Adams, and Wren left the room.

Secretary Zukert thanked the lawyers. "I apologize for interrupting your work. I much appreciate your cooperation. You're now free to return to your important duties. The janitors will put the tables and chairs back in their usual positions."

Rabbit told me later that Secretary Zukert had called on General Landon for that role because the military officers would not question his authority and because the Pentagon wanted the scandal to be contained at the highest level. Nonetheless, word spread, inevitably.

Reilly and I were escorted to another suite where, with a stenographer present, Rabbit took Reilly through a confirmation of his identification of Colonel Adams. Reilly affirmed that Adams was the man he had seen at Utowanna Lake and at Potter's, and he also stated that he had never before seen any of the other men in the line. The statement was typed and Reilly signed it.

I don't know where Adams was taken that day. Zukert, Adams, and Rabbit are all lawyers, so I'm sure that proper legal procedures were followed. Of course, Adams still hadn't confessed. He no doubt received all of his legal rights and not a bit more.

In the next few weeks, Rabbit and Wren brought the FBI in on the investigation of Adams. They found that he had bank accounts holding large sums—I don't know how much—and deposits in offshore banks. They also identified a dummy company tied to Adams, which he probably used for laundering money. So it appeared that he was in the spy business because it was lucrative, but he was also bitter about his career. He'd been passed over at his final opportunity for being promoted to general and was facing mandatory retirement. His co-workers said that he was unhappy. They also said that he had an inflated estimate of his ability.

Chapter Thirteen

Hastings found me at the hotel.

"Let's go for a ride in your car, Joseph, so we can have a private conversation. You drive. As you'll see, I've been drinking." He pulled a small bottle of vodka from the inside pocket of his jacket and offered it to me. "Have a nip?"

"No thanks." I looked for my car keys. "Where would you like to go?"

"Somewhere beautiful and pastoral. Somewhere quiet."

"Do I need to worry that you don't want to have witnesses around?"

"If I were going to do anything untoward, dear boy, I would not have been drinking. That would be unprofessional. Not to worry."

So I drove north out of Saranac toward Gabriels. Just after you pass Donnelly's ice cream stand there's a great view across the valley to mountains in the east, but Hastings didn't speak until we got to the potato fields by Split Rock Road. I stopped there. Ground mist settled on the field. We were in a valley, a flat stretch with mountains visible to the east, north, and west. The soil was a deposit of glacial debris, but you could grow potatoes in it.

He took a swallow from the vodka bottle and said: "You're not my friend, Joe. You're a man I met while doing a job. I don't have friends. I'm not in one place long enough to have them."

He was wearing a tie but he took it off and put it in his pocket. "It's a hit-and-run life, no pun intended. But an interesting life, better than a desk job. I suppose some people, most people, would say it's an exciting life. Sometimes it is. But I don't make friends. I do the job. Mostly I do it well. Sometimes I make mistakes." He took another small drink of the vodka, and again he offered it to me. I declined. "Trusting you is probably one of those mistakes." He put the cap on the bottle. "But I'm getting old.

"The kinds of things I do on the job," he said, "are not the things that make friends. I make enemies, not friends." He looked at the field and said, "Potatoes. Vodka is made from potatoes, or at least it can be." Hastings appeared to be looking at the rearview mirror. He adjusted it and then continued. "Are you really my friend, Joe? If I were good at my job, I'd doubt that. But why would I need friends? Why would I want them? What good would they be? I've thought about it. The answer I gave myself is that friends provide respect. And you need that. You need to have something to make you think that you're a decent person, that you deserve to live, that you're worth something. People fear me, but they don't respect me. So how can I respect myself?

"And I'm getting old. Have I said that? I don't think anyone is going to kill me, not yet. They'd have to be pretty smart and pretty quick. But when I retire, what would I do? Perhaps I could become a publican. And then one day, while I was pulling pints, an old adversary would come through the door. Perhaps it is just as well to stay sharp, to keep moving. And I've lost the few friends I once had. Friends die. Some of them die on the job."

I interrupted. "Like Vasily Rostov?" I wanted to change his

mood. He was dangerous when he was confident, but I thought he might be even more dangerous when he was depressed.

"Yes, well. That's the way it goes."

I said, "You don't regret Rostov's untimely departure." It was a statement, not a question.

"He misjudged the situation."

"The situation?"

"Yes, the situation. Very important to understand the situation. It's the essence of the whole thing, don't you see."

Hastings opened the car door, put one leg out, then turned and spoke again. "You don't seem very sympathetic today, old boy. I'm rather disappointed in you. Why are you cross with me?" He brought out the vodka bottle again. "Have a drop of this. Perhaps it will cheer you up."

I kept after him. "I never know what to make of you. You change by the minute."

"Adaptation is the key to survival."

"I thought the key was understanding the situation."

"That too, that too."

"You are full of bullshit, Hastings."

"No, not full. I've room for yet more. Would you care to give me some of yours?" He took two or three steps in the field, then returned to the car, shut the door, and said, "Chilly."

As we left the potato field, I turned onto the main road back to Saranac, the way we had come. This time Hastings commented on the mountains, noting that they were beautiful in the afternoon light. But as we approached Donnelly's, he said, "Stop for ice cream."

I said, "You don't like ice cream."

He said, "I have fancies."

So we stopped.

We each had a small vanilla cone. He ate only half of his. Then we resumed the trip back to Saranac, now only ten minutes away. As we neared town and passed Aubuchon Hardware, Hastings said, "Turn."

I was surprised. I said, "Why?"

He said, "Just turn."

So I took a sharp left onto a small street going up the hill. After I had made the turn and shifted down for the hill, I said, "Why?" again.

In a low voice he mumbled, "Don't look. Don't look in your rearview. Don't turn your head. Just proceed." I did.

There was a car behind us. It stayed with us. I said, "What now?"

Hastings spoke louder: "That car behind us, it followed us when we left the potato field. I didn't like it. That's why we stopped for ice cream."

"How do you know it's the same one?"

"It's the same. It's changed plates, changed from New York to New Jersey, different number, but it's the same car. Same make, same model, same color, same tinted windows. We've been made."

"What?"

"That car pulled out of the big hardware store as we went past. Then it turned and followed us up the hill."

"Maybe they live here."

"No, they don't. Stop."

I did. As soon as we stopped, he got out and stood in the middle of the road facing the oncoming car. I thought it was going to hit him. But it braked sharply, stopped, and then executed a quick U-turn. Hastings just stared it down. He wasn't holding a gun.

When he got back in the car, I asked him, "What in the hell was that?"

He growled, "The bastards don't trust me." His eyes were moving constantly, covering the road, the bushes, the houses, all of it. He said, "Are you armed?"

"No."

"You should be."

Then he didn't want to talk more.

I suppose if I had been driving that other car, I would also have done the quick U-turn. To this day I don't know whether the car was the one that followed us from the potato field, but Hastings sure thought it was. Was his memory good enough to record every detail about the car, even with the vodka? And was his eyesight good enough to see it all? I don't know. His memory and his powers of observation were remarkable. I'm not sure about the eyesight.

* * *

That evening Linda and I had a long-awaited date, but too much of it dealt with business. I'm afraid that at this point in our relationship our conversations focused on investigations more often than on romance. We both regretted it, but not enough to stop doing it. For a time I felt guilty about occupying our time together by going over the latest news about Reilly, Adams, and Hastings, but then I realized that she was just as interested in it as I was. We were real partners.

She started the conversation. "Now that Wren and Rabbit and also the top people in the Pentagon are all convinced that Colonel Adams was the mole, how does that change the way we think about Bill Reilly?"

I gave it a try. "Well, I don't think it means that Adams was the only spy. He may have been, he probably was, the principal one, but we know that Reilly gave data to the Soviets. I saw him put the microfilm into the letterbox. So Reilly isn't off the hook, but he may get some consideration or reduction in charges because he helped us nail Adams."

She picked up on the last point. "Yeah. He told us about Adams and then identified him. Reilly gave us Adams. Without Reilly's information, we wouldn't have caught the guy. Did Reilly negotiate a reduction in the charges against him in return for his cooperation?"

"No, we couldn't do that. It would've damaged the credibility of his ID if we had promised him a reward."

"So why did he help us?"

"Your feminine wiles. I think you persuaded him that it was in his best interest to provide us with another suspect."

"Yeah, and that, by itself, ought to be enough to cast doubt on Reilly's testimony."

"That's true, but I think Adams will fold. We now know that the phony data he had access to went to Moscow, and Mr. Potter can place Adams in the Adirondacks at the time Reilly said he was there, and he has a lot of unexplained money. That corroborates Reilly's account. Adams didn't have any reason to be in the Adirondacks except to meet with Kuznetsov. We've got him."

"Okay, so Adams is guilty, and Reilly is also guilty but maybe less guilty. Where does that leave us?"

"It leaves me thinking about the murder of Kuznetsov. We know with reasonable certainty that Reilly and Adams both had a connection to him. Reilly admits that he met with the man he called 'Dr. Lien'." So, if we know that both Reilly and Adams are connected to Kuznetsov, who had the better reason to kill him?

She complicated it, justifiably. "What about Hastings and Rostov?"

"Okay, right. But I don't see their motive. So let's just concentrate on Reilly and Adams for now and see what we come up with."

"Fair enough. How do we do that?"

"I've been wondering about how Reilly would react to seeing Kuznetsov meet with an unknown man in an out-of-the-way place, a man he later sees in an Air Force uniform. It looked like a secret meeting. Why would Kuznetsov do that? What would Reilly think?"

"The Air Force uniform would suggest that the meeting of the two of them had something to do with the TFX."

"Yeah, it probably would, or at least Air Force business. And Reilly already knew that Kuznetsov/Lien wanted info about the TFX. So what does that make the guy in the uniform?"

Linda said, "Probably another source of TFX information."

"I agree. And if Kuznetsov already had Reilly as a source, why would he need another source?"

"For different information, or better information, I suppose."

"Again I agree." This was going well, I thought. "Now, if Kuznetsov has another source, why would Reilly be concerned about that? Well, maybe the third man's information was better, more important, as you said. Adams was a Colonel, a high-ranking officer."

Linda cautioned me. "Reilly says he didn't know what the eagle on the shoulder meant."

"I don't believe that. And Adams is about twice Reilly's age, so probably a man of some importance. What does that suggest?"

"Reilly recognizes that the third man is a honcho. Highly placed."

"Right," I said. "So Reilly knows, we think, that Kuznetsov has both a highly placed source, somebody not from this area because he has to stay overnight at Potter's, and also a low-level draftsman source working at the mine."

Linda made the next step. "So now you're back to wondering why Kuznetsov would need the second source. What use would the low-level source be? And maybe Reilly wondered the same thing."

"Yep. A month ago we had a conversation at the Full Moon and you suggested that Reilly might be a 'feint', something intended to distract attention from the real attack. So maybe Reilly's function was to appear to be the source of the data but Adams was really the source of the important part."

Linda smiled another of her halfway smiles. "So I'm a great military tactician. Reilly was a sort of cover for Adams. We went after Reilly but overlooked Adams."

"And this tells us why Kuznetsov was in the Adirondacks. We wondered why he was here. Kuznetsov was visible—even having lunch at the hotel with Reilly. Surely he knew that we were watching his movements. He wanted to be seen. He was a little too obvious about it, over-eager, probably because if you have a well-located mole you certainly want to leave him in place, protect him. Moles are hard to develop."

"But people like Reilly can be sacrificed."

"Sure."

Linda said, "And if you were Reilly, how would you feel about that?"

"Of course his reaction depends on whether he had figured

it out. But I'll bet he was giving the situation at least as much thought as we have."

"So Reilly was probably plenty pissed off."

"Yeah."

Then once again Linda asked the right question. "A motive to kill?"

"Well, a motive for a serious argument anyway, which might lead to a killing."

But Linda had a somewhat different theory. "Or maybe Kuznetsov figured that leaving Reilly alive was a risk. You'd already seen Reilly use the dead drop at the cemetery, so he was no longer of use. We were on to him. And that created a risk that he would talk."

I asked, "So, in your story, what happened then?"

"Maybe they had a gunfight and Reilly won."

But I had found the body and there was no gun. "Kuznetsov wasn't armed."

"Maybe Reilly took the gun before he dumped the body. Or he disarmed Kuznetsov."

I didn't think so. "It's pretty hard to disarm somebody holding a loaded weapon. I don't know whether there was a paraffin test on Kuznetsov's hands to determine whether he had fired a gun recently. I could check that. But, in any of those scenarios, that would still be a killing done by Reilly. That's where this leaves us."

"Is there enough evidence to charge him?"

"For espionage, yes, pretty clearly enough. For homicide, probably not. We have a theory about a motive, but nothing solid. We can't place him at the scene of the killing, and we can't connect him to the murder weapon. We know he was willing to use a gun—he shot at Rostov, but that was self-defense. Not enough for homicide. But Hastings might have all he needs."

"What do you mean?"

"The death of a comrade-at-arms."

Linda raised her lovely eyebrows. "Do you think Hastings feels much comradeship with the Comrades?"

"No, but I think that was why he was sent here. Payback. Revenge."

*　*　*

Hastings came to see me the next night and we went to dinner at the Full Moon. He said, "Linda and I had a talk after school. She's a charming woman. You are a lucky man. She was reasonably discreet, you'll be happy to know, but after a bit of blather she warmed to the topic and she told me, in effect, that the two of you had figured it out. She was pleased."

"What do you mean?"

"Come now, old boy, you were a bit slow on this but I invited you to think about it, and now you have, and we all came to the same conclusion."

"Which is?"

"Dear, dear. This lack of trust. Come now. The obvious conclusion is that Colonel Kuznetsov was using Reilly to shield Adams, and Reilly rather understandably took offense at that."

"And?"

"And so Reilly killed him."

I asked, "Just like that?"

"Just like that. Perhaps in a fit of rage. Rather unprofessional, but it happens."

"It's just a theory, Ev. We don't have real proof. For Christ's sake! You can't act on this."

A gray-haired lady at the table next to us gave me a shocked look—actually, maybe closer to horrified. I'm not sure whether it was the 'Christ' or the 'killed him' that did it. Hastings smiled at her. He may have hoped she'd think we were joking.

"Sure I can."

"And what do you propose to do about it?"

"I will do my duty."

"As you see it."

"As my masters see it. You and I are mere employees, dear boy, not policy makers."

"I don't blindly follow orders."

"No, not blindly. But you do follow orders. How many times have you actually had to make the choice?"

"I'm new at this game."

"Quite."

"I can't just let you kill Reilly."

The gray-haired lady got up and moved. She hadn't finished eating. So I helped her with her chair and her coffee cup and said, "Just a rehearsal for a play, madam."

Then Hastings adopted his thoughtful pose. As usual, it meant that something facetious or whimsical was coming. "The masters of the institution for which I work believe it is unwise to let a deliberate homicide of one of our comrades pass without appropriate recompense or equilibration. They want satisfaction. That is their policy."

"Equilibration?! What in the hell does that mean?"

"I don't know, but it was a word on the spelling test. As was 'recompense'."

"Have you lost your marbles?"

"We must take note of the small, enjoyable things in our work, Joseph. We must find ways to brighten the day."

"Was there really a spelling test?"

"What does it matter? It was so long ago." Hastings paused and pulled down the cuffs of the keeper's jacket. "There certainly was an examination at the academy of the Special Operations Executive, where I received my professional education. I recall that there was a question about the best strategies to use when you face various sorts of dangers in the field. Several possible answers were supplied for each. You were to decide whether one strategy was better than another and you had to compare them—whether (B) was better than (C), and whether (D) was better than both of those or only one of them, and so on. The instructions were very complicated and hard to read. There were a great many options, possibilities. Trainees who struggled through it and provided answers were sent down. Those who left it blank were recruited. I crumpled the paper into a ball and threw it into a dustbin. I was graduated with colors flying. Anyone in the field who took the time to consider the options would be dead." Hastings leaned back in his chair. "You mustn't be so literal, Joseph". He signaled to the waitress that he wanted another beer. "That's a very American trait. Or maybe German." Then he paused again and added, sadly, "There are so many Germans in the United States."

On his way out of the restaurant, Hastings stopped at the lady's table and said, "You must come to see the play." She didn't respond.

Chapter Fourteen

Once again I arranged a meeting with Hastings. We avoided the Full Moon because we didn't want to scare any more old ladies. I suggested that we talk in my hotel room or at his motel, but he said the KGB had probably bugged both of those places. I thought he was imagining things, but I couldn't say that. So we went for a drive, but he said we couldn't talk in the car because that might also be bugged. He wanted an open place where it would be difficult for someone to get close to us without being seen. We couldn't use the high school football field because there were people around. So we talked standing on the beach at Axton landing. Odd choice of place, perhaps, but Hastings said there would be symmetry since this all started there. A strange reason, but Axton served our purpose. The approach is a one-lane road, and no one can get closer than about thirty yards from the beach without being seen. It was familiar territory for me. There was a light dusting of snow and no footprints.

I made my pitch. I told him that we, and he, didn't really have proof that Reilly had killed Kuznetsov. I said I didn't know who had done it or why. Hastings didn't disagree.

"You don't understand, Joseph. I don't greatly care whether Reilly killed Kuznetsov. I had no particular regard for the man. I'd met him once or twice, I suppose, but I didn't really know him. His death was not a tragedy. It was a consequence of his work, not unexpected, just as mine would be."

"Then why are you hunting Reilly?"

"The Kremlin wants him dead. Not because he's a person of consequence or importance. He isn't. But it is a question of trust. As I've said before, you have to understand the situation. The situation is that the KGB is here. Why are they here? I have asked them that. There are two men. I don't know them, but I've identified them and I confronted them. As I suspected, they were in the car that tailed us on the trip to the potato field. They were clumsy, and they know it. They say they were sent here to find Rostov, to track him, to determine what has become of him. I think that's partly true. They fear that he has defected. They want to know what happened to him because his defection would blow some of their operations, and then they would know that they should not rely on information coming from those. But it's also clear that they are worried about my loyalty. My defection would be a much bigger problem. I know more than Vasily did. I know about many operations in many places over many years."

"Why would they doubt your loyalty?"

"Look at it from their point of view. Somebody here killed Kuznetsov. Then Rostov disappears. Then Adams is arrested. A series of losses. And all while I'm here. They wonder what my role was in all of this. And then they see me meeting with you. They know who you are, of course, a CIA man. So rather understandably, they don't trust me. If Rostov's possible defection suggests to them that I might also be a risk to defect, they won't take that risk. They know that I transferred my allegiance from Britain to Russia. Would I transfer it back? They'll kill me first, without hesitation. I've been useful to them, but I'm fifty-one years old and I'm nearing the end of my usefulness for their purposes. The Order of Lenin and all of the other decorations

I've been awarded wouldn't save me. Not even close. So I need to establish that I can be trusted. One way to do that, or at least to begin the process, would be by killing Reilly. Again, it doesn't matter whether he's guilty. It's a test. The Kremlin knows that if I kill him it will be pretty obvious that I did it — or, if not, they will arrange to make it clear so that they will have something to hold over my head. Either way, they'll have something to use to control me. When they tire of me they could use me as trading material with your employers and send me back here to stand trial. That would keep me in line.

"Of course," Hastings continued, "I could kill the two KGB goons before they kill me — it would be easy enough. But then I'd be a hunted man. The KGB all over the world would come after me. I could try to disappear, but that isn't as easy as you may think. The Russians know that I have children and where they are.

"So that's the situation, Joseph, and it explains why it's important to understand the situation. I think the two men who are here would have killed me already, but they are afraid of me. My reputation gives me an advantage. And they don't speak much English — they are uncomfortable here. But I need to act soon."

At long last, he let me get a word in. "Are you troubled by the morality — or, I suppose, the immorality — of the work you do?"

"No. Are you?"

"Well, my work isn't the same as yours. I gather information, or try to, not very successfully, but you kill people."

"That seems to me simplistic, reductive, not to say unfair. I think of myself as dispensing justice, bringing order to the world, rather like a public servant."

"You're not serious."

"Of course I am. Would you rather I hadn't killed Vasily Rostov?"

"I've thought about it. I concluded that if you hadn't I wouldn't be here to think about it."

"There you are." Hastings accepted my gratitude. "And the world is a better place with you in it and him not."

"But don't you feel blood on your hands? Don't you regret the taking of life?"

"I'm not a vegetarian. I don't believe that all of God's creatures must die of old age."

"But you're talking about dumb animals, creatures without sense or decency or human worth."

"I couldn't think of a better description of Vasily Rostov."

I threw up my hands. I assume that the expression on my face was some version of disgust. And I was embarrassed by my stupidity. The way I had framed the argument gave him a fat target. I should have seen it. But as it turned out, he was somewhat chastened. He offered an explanation—not a *mea culpa* exactly, but a more serious explanation.

"As you may have guessed, or as your employers may have told you, I didn't go to university. My education was spotty. It has been filled-in a bit since, but not enough. I left school and needed a job. I was young and essentially unskilled, but I'd been raised on a farm in Yorkshire and the woods nearby provided some of our food. Then I was approached by a recruiter for H. M. Special Operations Executive. He had seen me on a firing range where I posted a good score. It was wartime. Mr. Churchill was making speeches intended to move people like me to go kill the Boche—the 'finest hour' and all that. it was put to me that the work was my patriotic duty.

"The job I'm doing now is simply an extension of that—for

a different employer, to be sure, but it's essentially the same work. Does the morality of it change when the employer changes? You may think so. I don't. The Kremlin and Whitehall and the Pentagon and Langley have different ideas about where virtue lies, but which one of them holds the truth? To me, it was a job. It provided employment. It still does."

"What about kindness, sympathy, decency? Is there no need for decency?"

"Of the Kremlin, Whitehall, the Pentagon, and Langley, which one hires people to distribute decency or kindness?"

So I gave up, reluctantly. We got in the car. It was snowing, and the wind was coming up. I didn't want to get stranded at Axton but I knew that the Coreys Road is plowed regularly because the Rockefellers have a place at the far end and they keep it open. When we got to the top of the Axton lane, at the point where the lane joins the road, we found the way blocked by another car.

Hastings grabbed my arm. "Stop!"

Actually, I didn't have much choice. There was no alternative, but Hastings had assumed command.

He said, "I didn't see them tailing us. I'm getting sloppy. Stupid old man."

I was wearing a long wool overcoat. Hastings said, "Do you have a gun hidden in those robes?"

"No."

"Is there a weapon in the car?"

"No."

"So I'll be one gun against two. So be it!" He pulled his pistol from a jacket pocket and released the safety. "I think I should consult you about this because if I die they will surely kill you. They couldn't leave you alive." He put on yellow-tinted shooting glasses that reduce haze. They also have an intimidating effect. "There are two possibilities: either we talk to them or I try to kill them both. I think there's a good possibility that I could do that. But then we'd have two dead Russians to dispose of. That would be messy and inconvenient, and there would certainly be reprisals. And if I shoot at them and don't get the job done, they will kill both of us. Even if we talk to them, of course, they may still decide to kill us. So tell me what you want to do. We don't have time to debate it."

I'm not really sure what I said then, but I think the point of it was that I preferred talking.

Hastings replied. "Okay, but it will have to be in Russian. So I'll do the talking. You get as low in the car as possible. You want the engine block between you and their guns. If I'm killed, you might try playing dead, but I don't think it will work."

Then he rolled down the passenger window and shouted something in Russian. There was a reply from the other car. I understood none of it.

Hastings rolled his window back up and opened the door. At the same time, a door of the other car opened. Hastings got out, put his feet on the ground, but stayed behind the open door as much as possible. He held his pistol in his left hand, shielded by the door.

From what I could tell, the other car did the same thing — one man out, shielded by an open car door. We were somewhere between ten and twenty yards away from them. It was hard to estimate. I couldn't see much because I had tried to get down onto the floor of the car.

There was more talking. Russian is not an especially mellifluous language, at least not as it was spoken that day. The conversation didn't seem to be going well. I heard Reilly's name once or twice. Then I heard it again.

Suddenly, before I was ready, Hastings was back in our car and the other car was driving away. I asked what happened. He told me he had promised to kill Reilly and to do it soon. He said he realized that this would give the KGB control over him, and he wasn't happy. Both he and the Russians knew that he could stall and not do it, but both also knew that that would lead to another confrontation and there would be shooting next time. He said the KGB didn't know I wasn't armed. They probably assumed I was manning guns, probably automatic weapons aimed at them. He laughed just a little. Neither side had been eager to start shooting.

I think his professional pride had suffered. Word would get around that he was losing his grip. He clearly would have preferred to kill them both. I don't know how much of his choice to talk was attributable to my presence and my inability to defend myself. I was a little ashamed to be a useless impediment cowering on the floor of the car. Maybe more than a little.

While all this was going on, not one car went by. We were in the Adirondacks.

* * *

Worrying about Hastings killing me had been bad enough. Now I had to worry about him killing Bill Reilly. Was that an improvement? Perhaps. But it was worrisome, nonetheless.

Linda and I weren't sure whether Hastings was cracking up. I suggested that he could be playing games, maybe testing me. Linda thought the mood swings might be a usual thing with Hastings—she saw signs of manic-depressive behavior patterns. The vodka was pretty clearly self-medication. We agreed on that. I wondered aloud whether his anxiety might be a result of stress produced because he was going to kill Reilly, soon. I also thought, but didn't say, that I didn't see any anxiety in him before he killed Rostov. Now, however, unlike then, he knew the KGB was watching him. That could make a difference. But Hastings had been in this business a long time. If he had killed as many people as his reputation suggested, he should be comfortable with it by now. Which was not entirely a reassuring thought.

Was preventing Hastings from killing Reilly really my job? I wasn't a cop. But I was sure as hell involved in the situation—"the situation," as Hastings put it. It seemed to me that I had some responsibility, maybe even a duty. There were only four people in Saranac who knew who Hastings was and what he was capable of. I knew, Linda knew, and the two guys in the car knew, but they weren't going to stop him. And Hastings had actually told me what he intended to do.

I didn't think I could just sit, keep quiet, and let Hastings do his thing. Was that what he expected me to do? If so, I took it as an insult. I thought Bill Reilly had probably killed Kuznetsov, but I couldn't prove that or even be sure of it. In any event, Hastings wasn't entitled to execute him.

But what should I do? I couldn't put Hastings under arrest. I didn't have police powers, and even if I had them he'd never let me do that. He'd resist. He certainly knew how. And he hadn't really done anything yet except talk. Well, actually, he *had*—he'd killed Rostov, but I was involved in that and in concealing it. It was probably better to let that lie.

Saranac Lake had a few police, not many, and so did the county. They were small-town cops. They didn't deal with internationally infamous assassins. If I went to the police and told them about Hastings and his threat, or musings, or whatever they were, what would have happened then? Their first thought would be that I was nuts. Their second, if I managed to persuade them to get that far, would be panic: "Holy shit! What do we do now?" And Hastings wouldn't surrender to them any more than he'd surrender to me. He'd fight. And the cops would be overmatched. More people would die that way than if I just let him go ahead and kill Reilly.

In the great scope of world affairs—of the relationship between the United States and the Soviet Union, the Cold War—Bill Reilly was chickenfeed. Nobody had ever heard of him. Who gave a damn? But it was happening on my turf. I cared. I couldn't just let it go.

Maybe I could call in the troops. Or try to. I knew I had to report to Rabbit, or that I should. Anything after that would be his call, not mine. That was attractive—but, like the police, it would probably result in a greater number of deaths. What would Rabbit's options be? He could hand it off to the FBI. He couldn't mobilize a CIA strike force because the CIA is not supposed to be involved in domestic law enforcement—it certainly wouldn't want a shootout in a small town. And, again, Hastings hadn't actually done anything (that is, anything I could tell Rabbit about).

So I called Rabbit to seek advice or, perhaps, a directive. I told him that Hastings had threatened to kill Reilly. But Rabbit was skeptical. "We don't have actual proof that Reilly killed the Russian, and I don't see how it would be possible for Hastings to have proof. I think he's bluffing."

"Does Hastings bluff?"

"Why not? Everyone else does."

"But why would he do that?"

"Maybe he wants to light a fire under you, to get you to panic and get Reilly arrested. The effect of that would be to make us invested in the proposition that Reilly was the spy. If the leaks of TFX info to Moscow came from Reilly, that might even be enough to get Colonel Adams acquitted. There's a flaw in that logic, but a defense lawyer could use it to create reasonable doubt. So maybe they could save their guy. Pretty clever move."

"So should I just do nothing?"

"Not exactly nothing, but we need to be careful, as always. You clearly can't use force to prevent Hastings from acting. Number One, he's a very dangerous adversary. He might kill you. Number Two, and more important, I don't want to disturb the status of diplomatic relations between the United States and the Soviet Union. That would be extremely costly. The Soviets are already upset because of the death of Kuznetsov and the disappearance of Rostov. We don't want more trouble. We're walking on eggshells here. So use your words. Talk. I know you've tried to persuade him, but try again."

* * *

Hastings and I had agreed to meet in the restaurant of my hotel the next morning at 10 A.M. I kept the appointment. He didn't. So I went looking for him. He wasn't at the motel. The office told me that he had checked out early in the day. I wanted to ask Linda where she thought he might be, but she was teaching and I'd missed her lunch hour. I'd have to wait until school was out. I didn't think I would find him in a bar in the middle of the day. That wasn't his style. After many years of operating in the field, Hastings didn't ordinarily seek companionship. But it occurred to me that he might have gone looking for the KGB, or they for him. Hastings could have been on the run from them, but that also didn't seem like his style. And then I wondered whether the KGB men were still alive. So I went back to my hotel room and waited for Linda's help.

As soon as I put the question to her, she said, "I bet he's gone to Newcomb or Long Lake to watch Reverend Mordecai. Hastings thinks that's the way to find Reilly."

"Damn. You're right!" I put my coat on. "I'd better get going. I don't want him to find Reilly. Quite apart from simple humanity, we may need Reilly to testify that he saw Adams meeting with Kuznetsov."

Linda had to take care of William, so she didn't go with me. It was possible that William might have enjoyed the drive, but there was a small risk that the errand might become dangerous. It was better for him to stay at home. Linda was frustrated, maybe even a little angry, that she couldn't go along. She likes action, and she has courage. Her reaction was a bit like her tennis — she's a risk-taker and somewhat impulsive. But there was no one else available to care for William.

So I drove down to Long Lake and then on to Newcomb. At the hotel, at Northern Borne, and at a couple of other grocery stores, I asked whether they had recently seen an English gentleman, and I described him. No luck. I went to Reverend Mordecai's church and asked the same questions. Again, no luck. No English gentleman. Mordecai also said he hadn't seen Reilly and didn't know where he was. That fine Christian clergyman may have been telling the truth, but I wasn't counting on it. I went back to Saranac.

At my hotel, I found a message from Hastings. It said, "You have been inquiring about me." And then it gave a telephone number. I still didn't know where he was. He was hiding—not from me, I think, but he didn't want trouble.

So I called him and he suggested that we meet for a drink at the Bide-a-Wee.

Chapter Fifteen

The Bide-a-Wee is a roadhouse in Raybrook, located near Saranac on the route to Lake Placid. On the outside, it's a nondescript, low-slung post World War II brown building, but on the inside it has an exuberant pan-British theme, primarily Scottish, I suppose, but with elements from England, Ireland, and Wales. Hastings found it amusing. He said, "You'd never see anything like this in the U. K." There's a large, framed collection of three-inch square swatches of fabric displaying the tartans of numerous clans, an Irish harp made of plastic (or maybe cardboard), and a picture of a Yeoman Warder of the Tower of London, possibly cribbed from a Beefeater's gin advertisement. Standing in the corner is a genuine plaster cast of the statue of Gelert, the loyal and tragic dog of Welsh legend who saved a baby from a wolf, but was killed when the child's father thought the dog had killed the infant. The Wee is an inspiring yet cozy sort of place.

Hastings asked me to invite Linda to join us there for a social occasion, and I did. He was now in a better mood. He didn't explain why. Linda and I drove in separate cars because she would need to pick up William later.

We were on our second Guinness when Hastings said, "Now that we know each other well, I think I can tell you that Hastings is merely a work name."

I said, "You're widely known by that name."

"Yes. Well, I've used it a long time. But my surname is Hatter-Hatton. Don't laugh."

Linda made the only gracious reply that was possible. "It's an unusual name."

He formed the fingers of his two hands into a church steeple. "Somewhat repetitious, I know. My ancestors only married their cousins."

Linda again. "Did your people make hats?"

"Probably. Way back, they probably did."

I said, "Where did the other name come from?"

"About seven generations ago, one of my ancestors got tired of being a Hatter so he started calling himself Hatton. His descendants kept that name. So there were two branches of the family, the Hatters and the Hattons, and then my grandmother and grandfather, one from each of the two branches, married and joined the two, creating the double-barreled name."

Linda was worried about inbreeding. "So you are your own cousin?"

"At some quite distant remove, yes I am."

She followed-up, "What sort of work do the Hatter-Hattons do now?"

"Oh, they're mostly clergymen – some are Church of England but others are more original."

I was practical. "What should we call you?"

He didn't hesitate. "I prefer Hastings. Better yet, Ev."

As was often the case, Linda was fascinated by Hastings's clothing. Because the weather was cold, he was wearing the keeper's jacket. The very heavy tweed was perfect for a cold night in the Adirondacks. She said, "That's a serious coat you're wearing. It could take some punishment."

He agreed, "Yes, I'm afraid it already has. The wool looks

thick enough and tightly-woven enough to be bullet-proof, but I'm afraid it isn't really."

Then the conversation changed. Linda left to get William and take him home, and Hastings and I moved to a more secluded table. It was a gangster table—in a far corner with solid walls on both sides and a clear view of the door so we could see anyone entering. We talked business.

When I asked Hastings if he had had more trouble with the KGB men, he just waved his hand dismissively, as if they were of no consequence.

I said, "Ev, if you kill Reilly, the police and the FBI will come down on you and I'll have to help them."

"It's my job."

"And my job is to protect him."

"He's earned it. He killed Kuznetsov. There are consequences."

"You don't know for a fact that he did it."

"In my line of work, we don't need proof beyond a reasonable doubt. You may not be satisfied, Joseph, but I'm satisfied." He tightened the knot of his tie. Getting into uniform, I thought. "Ask Rabbit for his professional judgment. I'm sure he'll tell you he wants Reilly as a witness if the Adams case goes to trial, and he will recognize that as a good reason for me to kill him. He'll agree with me. It's my job. Where is your appreciation for duty?"

"My duty is to prevent you from doing it."

"I hope you won't try." Hastings stood. "By the way, you'd need to carry a gun in order to stop me."

It was a good thing that we had two cars. I don't know what might have happened if we had driven to Saranac together.

* * *

I was clearly making no progress in trying to persuade Hastings to let Bill Reilly live. I consulted Linda. I told her about the two KGB men, but I didn't give her the details about the standoff at Axton. Linda was alarmed that the KGB was here, so I asked her why they were any more scary than Hastings, a professional assassin. She said that she knew Hastings; he was a real person. Then she said something about how the unknown horror or the inchoate dread was more terrifying, harder to deal with, and that was why ghost stories and tales about inhuman creatures were scary, and the KGB seemed like that.

I thanked her for this insight, but I thought my problem was ignorance about how to keep Reilly alive. She observed, sensibly enough, that a good first step would be to find him and warn him. Granted. But where was he?

She said, "He's gone underground."

I said, "Underground."

She looked at me and I looked at her. We were thinking the same thing.

Reilly had worked at the mine. He certainly knew about the old tunnels built for the nineteenth century ironworks. A map of the tunnels was one of the things on the microfilm Reilly left at the cemetery for Kuznetsov to pick up.

The tunnels would not be a pleasant place to live, but someone was trying to kill Reilly and he knew that. Presumably, the someone was Hastings. There had been a near miss at Gananoque. Somebody certainly shot at him. If Reilly knew that the two KGB men were here , that would also frighten him. That could be enough to drive him into the tunnels. Maybe some part of them was barely habitable. He knew more about the tunnels than we did.

The Opalescent River and the North Branch of the Hudson

run down from the high peaks past the mine and the abandoned village called Adirondac. In the spring, when the snow melts, a torrent of water comes down. The pressure of the water washes out the banks of the rivers, changes their courses, and cuts away parts of the hills. Over the one hundred and twenty years since the tunnels of the iron mine were built, the rivers have excavated enough of the land to expose some of the tunnels. There are now new entrances where the covering earth and rock washed away. Entrances to the mine, in effect, open and close from year to year.

Much of the iron ore is still there. It looks like grey rock streaked with rust. The rust is the iron. Titanium is mixed in, but I don't know how to spot it. The walls of the mine are solid rock. Where they haven't been damaged by floods and decades of erosion, they might be pretty dry.

When I arrived at the mine, I saw that Hastings's rental car was already there, and then I found him nearby. Either he had the same thought we did, or he had followed Reilly to the mine.

I asked Hastings, "Is he here?"

"I think so, but I haven't seen him."

"Where are you going to look?"

"In the tunnels."

"Where's the entrance?"

"Down the hill, along the banks of the river, you see several openings. Some are covered by brush and overgrowth, but you can find them if you look. I've explored."

"What are you going to do?"

"I'm going in."

"That's dangerous. It'll be dark and he knows those tunnels better than you do. This is his territory. He'll have the advantage."

"Oh ye of little faith. I have the advantage of experience. This won't be the first time I've gone hunting in a tunnel."

"Why not just stay here and wait him out? He'll have to go for food sometime."

"There are too many openings. Holes where the tunnels have caved-in. I think he could get out without being seen."

"Why are you doing this? Come with me to Langley. I'll escort you. I'm sure they'd be glad to employ you. What you know is worth a fortune."

"There'd be no way they could protect me."

"The people at Langley have a lot of skills. They could give you a new identity. You could settle down and have a great life."

"I doubt it. Under the right conditions and circumstances, anybody can kill anybody. It isn't hard to do. Remember that, Joe."

"Let's just go talk to Langley."

"No, I don't think I'll do that. I think I'll just go back to Europe, or perhaps South Africa or Australia, and if I return to this country it will be on a different passport and you'll no longer be standing in my way."

"Why won't I be in your way?"

"Well, you would be unwise to track me down, but that would depend on your own choices, of course. Or perhaps you will have retired, or be incapacitated."

"You wouldn't harm me, would you?"

"Don't count on it. I haven't survived this long by being foolish or sentimental." He paused. "You owe me a little, you know. Think of the late Vasily Rostov."

At that point, I saw Linda's car arriving. I hadn't expected her, but she'd guessed where I'd gone. I went to meet her, and when I got back to my car Hastings wasn't there. It was pretty obvious that he went looking for Reilly, probably through one of those hidden entrances to the mine.

There was snow on the ground, but there were a lot of tracks and I didn't know which had been made by Hastings. The snow wasn't wet and there was a wind, so the tracks were covering quickly.

I picked the footprints that I thought were most likely to be his, and I followed them down the hill toward the river. It was November and the river was only a stream, maybe ten yards across, but you could see from the banks that it had been much larger in the spring. I worked my way along the river, looking up the hill as I went, trying to identify possible openings to the mine. The leaves were off the deciduous trees and plants, but most of the trees were conifers, primarily balsams, hemlocks, and white pines. I remember that the needles of the tamaracks had turned yellow, but hadn't yet fallen. Under other circumstances, the woods would have been beautiful.

I had to look closely because the brush was thick. I saw two gaps in the undergrowth, possible openings to the tunnels. I had to be careful because, as Hastings had told me, the roofs of the tunnels had caved. In some places, those cave-ins created small holes where you could break an ankle or a leg. In others, the holes were big enough to see, but I didn't want to get close to them because the edges were unstable and the hole could swallow my whole body, dropping me twenty feet or more to the floor of the tunnel. I moved slowly.

With considerable effort, I located two places where it looked like I could get access to a tunnel. At one of these, I'd have to crawl in on my hands and knees. At the other, I could walk in if I bent over. I chose the latter.

I worried about running into den-dwelling animals. There

are bears and wolves in the Adirondacks, but there aren't poisonous snakes because it's too cold. Of course, there would be bats.
Caves in the Adirondacks are full of bats, and you are grateful
for them from mid-May to mid-June because bats eat mosquitoes, but right then I was not much worried about mosquitoes.

I looked into the more accessible tunnel. It was dark in there.
I had a flashlight, and I used it to look for tracks in the sand on
the floor of the tunnel—tracks made by Hastings or Reilly or
animals.

I'd left Linda in the parking lot, but now I heard her coming toward me along the riverbank. I wanted her advice about
strategy and options, but I thought it was dangerous there and
I told her so. Her expression changed as I spoke, changing from
concentration and determination to something more aggressive.
We had an argument, right there in the snowy woods.

I said, "Go back to the parking lot."

She said, "Don't order me around. I'm an adult, and I'm competent. I know my own mind. I have a gun and I know how to
use it. I've hunted in these woods. My dad taught me how to
shoot when I was twelve years old. I know what I'm doing."

"I have my own gun. You should think of William. You're his
mother. He needs you."

"I've thought about William. Plenty. Far more than you
have, I'm sure. I love William. But I love you too, Joe. I won't
leave here. Don't worry about me. I'll be alright. I've lived in the
Adirondacks all my life and I'm not afraid of the woods. I know
how to move."

I conceded. She wasn't going to back off.

Then we heard gunshots inside the mine, and a human cry,
probably a cry of pain, but we couldn't tell where in the mine the
sounds were coming from. There was an echo, and there were so

many openings created by sinkholes and small entrances that some of the sounds seemed to be coming from behind us.

Linda started to go into the mine.

I said, "Are you nuts?"

"We can't just stay here and let them shoot each other."

"What if they shoot at you?"

"I'll call out, so they know it's me."

"Great! Then all they have to do is aim at the sound."

I think Linda believed that, if she was with me, neither Reilly nor Hastings would shoot at us. I didn't share her optimism. But she was trying to protect me.

In a rather ungentlemanly way, I'm afraid, I pushed Linda aside and entered the mine, crouched down. I went first, but Linda was right behind me. The tunnel was dark. It was hard walking because there was loose rock on the floor, and the farther in I went the darker it got. Several yards in, maybe thirty steps, I found a rusted iron track that had been used for hauling ore out the mine. I discovered the rails by tripping over them. So I turned on my flashlight. That was a mistake.

From far up ahead, I don't know how far, I heard Hastings's voice.

He said, "Back off, Joe. I know Linda is there. You don't want her to be hurt. Neither do I."

I started to protest, but he interrupted. "Joe, never hold your light in front of your body. It makes you a target. Remember that."

I was holding the flashlight in my left hand and my pistol in the right. As soon as I moved the flashlight farther to the left, he shot it out of my hand.

He also shot the hand. Only in cowboy movies can someone shoot something out of a hand without damaging the hand. I was bleeding, and a surgeon later told me some of the bones were broken. Without the flashlight, I couldn't see how bad the damage was, but it was painful. Hastings wasn't screwing around.

Luckily, Linda had not been in the line of fire. But she was furious. She shouted at him, "You rotten sonofabitch!"

He shouted back, "Not very ladylike, my dear."

Linda fired her pistol in the general direction of the sound of his voice. Her shot hit the rock wall and we saw sparks from the flint-like rock. At the same time, Hastings yelled. She hadn't hit him, but chips of the rock had.

He went quiet. So did we. We heard him scuffling along the floor. It sounded like he was moving farther back into the mine.

Linda was wearing a rough canvas jacket, but she took that off and tore a strip of cloth from her cotton shirt. She wrapped the cloth around my wounded hand and tied it tightly. She said, "Let's get the hell out of here. He's nuts."

I said, "He's wounded."

She said, "So what? He's still a killer. Leave him."

"I want to talk to him. I owe him something." She didn't know about Rostov.

"Let Hastings take care of himself."

We were speaking very quietly. I said, "What about Reilly? I can't just run away as soon as the shooting starts. I'm a professional. I'm trained for this." That last was an exaggeration.

I moved slowly ahead. There was no light. About twenty feet farther on, I tripped again. This time, the barrier was something soft. Now I was on my hands and knees. The sand was wet. Blood. The barrier was a body, the size of Bill Reilly. I could feel that he was wearing wool pants and a wool jacket, ready for roughing it, and I could also tell that he was quite dead. I crawled beside the body and found a pistol. So Hastings and Reilly had shot it out. But Hastings clearly got the better of it.

Hastings was ahead of me somewhere. If I stayed put and kept Reilly's body between me and Hastings, I would be safer. For a few minutes, I didn't move. I waited for Hastings to speak or shoot, but he didn't. I'm not sure how long I was there. I think time was probably passing slowly.

Then I decided that the defensive position wasn't accomplishing anything. I crawled in the general direction of Hastings, or toward where I thought he was. It was hard to crawl. The floor of the mine was mostly sand, but it included a lot of rocks, some of them sharp. It also wasn't level. There were dips and bumps. It's hard to crawl using only one hand, and my good hand was holding a gun. But the gun didn't get in the way much, and I used the heel of the broken hand.

About five minutes of tough crawling beyond the body, I found more fresh blood. This couldn't be from Reilly. It was too far away from him. And this wasn't where Hastings stood when Linda shot at him. So Reilly must have wounded him.

I called out to him. "Hastings, you're wounded."

"Indeed I am. More than once. It was dark. That's how he managed to get me before I killed him. Killed in self-defense, mind you, perfectly legal. And then you sprayed my face with small daggers. My face! I feel like St. Sebastian."

"What?"

"Never mind. I suppose he's a British saint."

"You're no kind of saint."

"But I'm an angel of mercy. I bring comfort to the afflicted. Blessed relief from their demons. And, too, I bring justice to the wicked."

"Where did he hit you?"

"In the thigh. Not far from my precious equipment—still precious even though not used much recently."

"Watch out for the femoral artery."

"If he hit the femoral artery, I'll be dead soon."

"How much blood is there?"

"It's everywhere. There's no stopping it."

"Let me get you out of here. You need help right away."

"Can't do that." He choked and coughed. "Have to play out my hand. Try your luck."

"Your voice sounds weak. I think you're fading out."

"Come on, Joe, you can take me. You've already cut up my face."

"That wasn't my shot. That was Linda."

"Oh, for God's sake, don't let that get out."

Then a large number of bats took off from the general direction of Hastings and flew toward the entrance of the tunnel. Something had spooked them. I couldn't see the bats, but the beating of their wings made a roar and created a breeze. Until I realized it was bats coming toward me, I froze. Bats weren't great, but knowing that it was bats was better than not knowing what the hell it was. Their radar works and they avoid you. I could hear Linda, still yards behind me, say, "Bats!" Then a piece of the roof fell, roughly five feet by ten feet. Earth came down with it and made a mound on the floor. The bats must have sensed it or have heard the stone crack.

I could see sky through the hole, and the new opening provided enough light for me to see Hastings leaning against a column of rock that had been left to support the roof. I think his weight against the column may have been enough to cause the crack.

As I watched, he slid down the column to the floor. He said, "I'm going, Joe."

I had difficulty hearing him, but a hard edge had come into his voice. I wasn't sure. I didn't know whether he was dying or was playing me. Then I decided to risk it.

I stood and walked over to him. He didn't move. His face had many small cuts, some of them with pieces of rock still in them. But his eyes were intact. He could see well enough to shoot. Then he looked at me and said, "Take good care of Linda. She's a sweetheart."

"Yes, she is."

"Tell her I forgive her for the damage to my face. Don't let her think she had anything to do with my death. She didn't."

"I'll tell her, but you're not dead yet."

"Yes, I am."

I sat down in the sand and rock beside him. I supported his head and shoulders. "Ev, I didn't want this to happen."

"I know." He tried to smile. "I didn't either." He grimaced. "And now we've spoiled the keeper's jacket. I wanted you to have it. But someone put a hole in it." Hastings took a deep breath and gritted his teeth. "In my papers, you'll find the name of a weaver who has mended it before." He tried to lift his head, but couldn't do it. "And there'll be bloodstains too." Very softly. "Try salt with vinegar." He closed his eyes and was gone.

Salt with vinegar. Later it occurred to me that those words should be on his gravestone. But I don't know if he'll have a marked grave. Who would bury him? The Soviets? Surely not the United Kingdom. Maybe the Hatter-Hattons. Was that really his name? What name would be on the stone? Who was he?

Chapter Sixteen

His flashlight was by his body. Mine was shot to pieces, but his worked. I picked it up and walked back to where Linda was, still near Reilly's body. I was glad to see that she was crying. Of course I knew she had real emotions and wasn't just a tough guy. There was more to her than that.

I said, "Since it seems that you and I will get out of this alive, will you marry me?"

"I think that would make me happy."

"Which part? Staying alive or marrying me?"

I kissed her, and I guess you could say that she kissed me too.

Linda and I walked to the office of the titanium mine and told the staff about the two dead bodies in the old tunnels. Police were called, and also an ambulance even though we had reported that we were sure the men were dead. We were right. But the ambulance was useful for transporting the bodies, and the medical technicians knew how to preserve evidence. Bright lights were set up in the mine and photos were taken before the bodies were moved.

Linda and I answered questions for three hours. The police wanted to know who Hastings was. I had to be careful about what I could say. Paraffin tests were done on our hands. I hadn't fired a weapon, but Linda had. She turned her pistol over to the cops for them to compare the ballistics to the bullets in the bodies. She hadn't hit any flesh, only rock. I told them that Linda was defending me. My wounded hand was Exhibit A. Then I called Rabbit from the mine's office, and he or someone at Langley intervened and assured the police that I was legit.

When the police finished with us, and I had gone back to Saranac, I called Rabbit again and gave him a preliminary report. The basic facts seemed pretty simple: Hastings and Reilly killed each other. Reilly died first, and then Hastings bled to death from wounds presumably inflicted by Reilly. Hastings had shot my hand and it would need surgery. Linda had fired toward Hastings after he shot me, but she didn't hit him. These were the facts as I knew them.

I was put on administrative leave pending a more complete report. Over the next day or two, Linda and I talked. Two things puzzled us: First, why was Hastings so certain that Reilly had killed Kuznetsov? What did he know that we didn't? Second, if Hastings killed Reilly in self-defense, as he claimed, then why was he so adamant about refusing to leave the mine, refusing to get medical help?

Linda and I debated these questions. On the second one, we had a number of theories. One was what I called the fatalism theory. Hastings had seen enough gunshots to know which wounds are fatal. He knew he was mortally wounded. If he wouldn't survive, why not ride it out, accept it calmly. Another theory was the retirement option—Hastings knew he was near the end of his career. He was at least somewhat depressed about that. His future probably didn't seem attractive. He was ready to go. A third theory was the valor motivation. He wouldn't have wanted to look weak. He liked being seen as a tough guy, and here was an opportunity to die with his boots on. It would add to the legend of Ev Hastings. These all seemed plausible.

And then the coroner's report came in. It suggested that perhaps Hastings did not, in fact, kill in self-defense. He might have faced a prosecution for murder. The coroner's physician found that Reilly was shot three times, twice in the head and once in the abdomen. The report concluded that the shot to the abdomen came first because either of the two head wounds would have killed Reilly instantly. The bullet to the stomach probably would also have been fatal, but he would have been able to shoot Hastings after that wound. One of the head wounds was an "execution shot" to the temple delivered at close range. It left powder burns. Reilly was probably already dead when that shot was fired. Of course, it was possible that Reilly had shot first and wounded Hastings, who then fired all three of the bullets that hit Reilly, but it was also possible that Hastings had fired the first shot. The evidence was inconclusive, but Hastings didn't know that.

The footprints in the mine and the locations of the pools of blood were thoroughly examined and analyzed. I had messed up the tracks by crawling through them, but the evidence that remained was consistent with the theory that Hastings had walked over to Reilly after he was already on the ground—as a result of the stomach wound and perhaps the first head wound—and then fired the execution shot.

The second pool of blood I found was, in fact, Hastings's blood. It's likely that he stood in that location for some time as Linda and I entered the mine, and he considered what to do with us. He was probably standing there when he shot my flashlight and hand.

So if Hastings had come out of the mine and lived, he might have had to stand trial. He would've wanted to avoid that. To escape from the mine and get back to his car, which he almost certainly knew he didn't have the strength to do, would have required him to kill both me and Linda. Not a likely or attractive option.

Rabbit agreed with all of this, but that still left the first question. Did Reilly kill Kuznetsov? Rabbit added a small piece of information. Kuznetsov had worked with Vasily Rostov and the two of them were friends. Both were on the Embassy staff. They were in this country on Russian passports as what are known as "legal spies"—that is, they had entered this country legally, as diplomats—unlike Hastings who was an "illegal spy," off the books. It was likely that Kuznetsov told Rostov about his trouble with Reilly. As we knew, after Kuznetsov's death Rostov had come to the Adirondacks to kill Reilly.

Rabbit said, "Soviet intelligence wanted to silence Reilly, to shut him up. Reilly's only purpose, given their objectives, was to protect Colonel Adams by providing us with an alternative source for the TFX leaks, but what convinces me that Reilly killed Kuznetsov is that the Russian didn't try to conceal his presence in the Adirondacks. He made no effort to avoid attracting attention. Even Reilly could see that Kuznetsov was in full view. And when he also saw that there was another American, Adams, feeding Kuznetsov, it all became clear to him.... Kuznetsov underestimated Reilly. He saw the draftsman at the mine as a simple sap. But Reilly had more moxie.... I wonder if Kuznetsov knew that Reilly was skilled with guns. I'll bet not. A fatal mistake."

Then Rabbit said, "What does Linda think about this?"

I said, "She agrees with you." I'm no fool.

"Good!" If it were possible to transmit a smile on a telephone line, I think I would have seen one.

A month later I read two small articles on the same page of the Saranac Lake newspaper:

Adirondack Daily Express, December 15, 1964, p. 6.
Coyle, Boudreau Wedding

On December 14, Linda Coyle of Saranac Lake married Captain Joseph Boudreau of the U. S. Air Force. Captain Boudreau formerly resided in Saranac Lake, and in recent weeks he has been here pursuing official duties.

The bride is the daughter of Helen and Michael Coyle of this village. Captain Boudreau is the son of the late Margaret and Alex Boudreau, also of Saranac Lake. The couple was attended by the bride's son, William, age 4, who served as best man and ring bearer.

The wedding ceremony was performed by Howard Rodgers, Justice of the Peace, in his chambers at the Village Hall. Following the wedding a reception for family and friends was held at the Hotel Saranac.

Mrs. Boudreau teaches in the Saranac Lake public schools. The location of their future residence will depend upon orders received from the U. S. Air Force.

—

Adirondack Daily Enterprise, December 15, 1964, p. 6.
Two Men Die at Lake Clear

On Sunday, December 13, the owner of a camp at Lake Clear found two dead men there. The house had been rented for a month. The bodies were in an advanced stage of decomposition, but the owner said that one of the men appeared to be the person who had rented the camp.

The men remain unidentified. Police are investigating. There were no signs of a struggle.

A plate of poisonous mushrooms was found on the kitchen table, cooked. Pending investigation, both deaths are presumed to have been accidental, due to mushroom poisoning.

No identification was found on the bodies. The owner of the camp said that the man who rented the house paid a month's rent in advance, in cash. The man had a "foreign accent," the owner said.

No automobile or truck was found at the camp, but the property is located near the Lake Clear railroad station and the residents could have walked.

The coroner found that the men had been dead for "quite some time, probably several weeks, as the weather has been cool."

"I'll be damned!"

Acknowledgments

I could not have written this book without the encouragement and advice of Callum Angus, William Conger, Dr. John Denby, Edward Laumann, J. Landis Martin, and Irvin Slate. My advisor on literary matters, Chris Angus, provided valuable criticism, as did my advisor on all things, Anne Heinz. I relied heavily on Anne's choices among alternative wordings. I owe a special debt to David Collins, a meticulous scholar of the English language, who identified every use of the past progressive tense and other impediments in the manuscript. (Joe's narration, however, is his own and it retains a few peculiarities that David Collins would flag.)

It was a pleasure to work once again with Linda Hughes, who did the editing for Deeds Publishing with an eagle eye and good humor. In Linda's honor, one of the major characters in the novel is named for her.

The maps were created by Catherine Zaccarine of Zaccarine Design, Inc., Chicago. I have worked with her on several previous projects and, as always, she did the work with art, imagination, and precision.

Deeds has now published two of my books. As before, the care, creativity, and skill of Bob Babcock, Mark Babcock, and Matt King made the novel a better book.

My thanks to all!

J. H., May 2020

About the Author

Jack Heinz has written on a variety of subjects: farm price supports (*Harper's Magazine, Yale Law Journal*); boxing (Sports Illustrated); modern art (Bruno David Gallery, Duane Reed Gallery); 19th century American history (*U. of Illinois Press*); classic jazz (*The Hudson Review*); the legal profession (university presses of Harvard, U. Chicago, and Northwestern); and political violence in the late 1960s (Deeds Publishing).

In his youth, Heinz spent many hours in the water. He was a lifeguard, swimming teacher, and waterfront director. He also led canoe trips in northern Wisconsin on the Namekagon, Couderay, and Flambeau rivers, which make a brief appearance in this novel. The Heinz family still has a half-dozen canoes, and he gets out on the Stony Creek Ponds among the loons in the summer, but he no longer attempts adventuresome journeys.

He is the Owen L. Coon Professor Emeritus at Northwestern University's Pritzker School of Law, an affiliated scholar at Northwestern's Institute for Policy Research, and a senior research fellow emeritus at the American Bar Foundation. He was an Air Force officer, serving in the Pentagon and the White House.